Puffin Books
Editor: Kaye Webb

The Golden Bird

There was once a dear, wise old woman named Babka who lived alone in a little house in the forest and made brooms for a living. All the villagers liked her, and the dogs and children too, but her chief friends were the wild birds, who would tap on the window calling her to feed them and sometimes take their food right from her fingers.

One day Babka found a poor bird lying on the ground exhausted with hunger, so she took it home and fed it and warmed it. Soon life and lustre came back to its plumage and its tail spread out like a fan of gold. It was indeed the King of Birds and it granted her three wishes for her kindness – that her forest home should never be spoilt, a fountain that never ceased to flow and a fire that never went out.

It was lucky indeed for Babka that she had won the friendship of the Golden Bird, for she needed it in the days to come when the wicked sorceress Queen cast a spell on her foster child, the Nut Maiden, famine struck the people and she had to journey far into the frozen north in search of a lost Grey Gander who would save the land from its misery.

This magical, beautiful book grew out of stories told to the author as a child by her Polish father, and it is perfectly matched by the illustrations by Jan Pienkowski, an artist who spent his childhood in Poland.

For readers of eight and over.

EDITH BRILL

THE
GOLDEN
BIRD

ILLUSTRATED BY

Jan Pienkowski

PUFFIN BOOKS

Puffin Books, Penguin Books Ltd,
Harmondsworth, Middlesex, England
Penguin Books, 625 Madison Avenue,
New York, New York 10022, U.S.A.
Penguin Books Australia Ltd, Ringwood,
Victoria, Australia
Penguin Books Canada Ltd, 41 Steelcase Road West,
Markham Ontario, Canada
Penguin Books (N.Z.) Ltd, 182-190 Wairau Road,
Auckland 10, New Zealand

First published by Dent 1970
Published in Puffin Books 1972
Reprinted 1974, 1976

Copyright © Edith Brill, 1970
Illustrations copyright © Jan Pienkowski, 1970

Made and printed in Hong Kong by
Sheck Wah Tong Printing Press

Set in Linotype Pilgrim

To Olive and Margery

Contents

Contents

Chapter One

The Three Wishes

Once upon a time there lived in the great forest of the western plain a broom-maker called Babka. Her little wooden house stood in a clearing and was surrounded by a garden where sunflowers grew almost as tall as the chimney. The walls were made of logs dovetailed at the corners, and the space between the logs was filled with moss and clay. Every spring Babka painted this filling with a special blue paint to keep it watertight. The steep roof was covered with larch shingles overlapping each other like fish scales and these had become a silvery grey with age. Indeed, the little house was so old it had become as much a part of the forest as the trees.

Babka too was old; her face was brown and wrinkled. But her blue eyes were bright. This was how the villagers had always known her; she never seemed to grow any older.

The village at the forest edge was quite a long way from the clearing. When the snow came Babka was cut off for weeks. It was a hard time, for in the brief hours of daylight she had to collect enough dead wood to keep her fire burning through the long cold nights. But when her friends in the village suggested she should stay with them through the bad months she only smiled and said she was very comfortable in her little house. She had her two goats, her hens and all the wild birds of the forest for friends, and never felt lonely.

In the spring and summer she looked after her garden, in the autumn she gathered her harvest of potatoes, beans and onions and stored them away in the loft, while in the winter she gathered fuel. All the year round she made her brooms, selling them in the villages and farms.

Everybody knew Babka in her faded blue skirt, flowered jacket and apron. In cold weather she draped an old russet shawl over her head and shoulders, and her figure became bunchy with extra petticoats. The fierce farm dogs never barked at her, and the children came running to show her their toys. The villagers gave her butter, or a little pot of honey or a newly baked honey cake in return for the salves and medicines she made from the herbs of the forest.

But Babka's chief friends were the wild birds. They came to her without fear. The tiny goldcrest was never alarmed when she peeped into the nest hanging like a cradle beneath the spruce boughs, the siskins and redpolls and titmice would flit from bough to bough above her head as she walked in the forest, chattering in their shrill tinkling voices. The nuthatches, woodpeckers and tree-creepers would call gaily as they ran up and down the branches, and she would stop and smile at their quick movements and soft plumage. She never tired of watching them. Two robins might seem alike to most people, but Babka knew one from the other as easily as she would know two children.

Before the door of her hut was a dead tree-trunk with bare outstretched branches, and on this she hung fat and bones. If they were very hungry the birds would tap on the window calling to her to feed them. Sometimes they would not wait while she filled the birch-bark tray with crumbs and seed but would take the food from her fingers, hovering about her like a rainbow of leaves. And when they had

finished feeding they would perch on the old tree and puff out their feathers, preening themselves and chirruping. Babka loved to hear their contented voices.

One day in late autumn when she was gathering wood some distance from her hut she saw two strangers riding through the forest. Babka quickly hid behind a clump of bushes to wait until they had passed. Since their good King had vanished mysteriously one evening when walking alone in the palace gardens the people of the forest had learned to fear strangers. It was safer to keep out of sight of them. They might be spies of the Queen, who had seized the throne when the King disappeared. She was a wicked, greedy woman who had made herself so powerful that nobody dared whisper against her, for her punishments were cruel. It was believed she was a witch, and not only used witchcraft to make the King disappear but held the Prince, their son, in an enchantment which made him helpless to act against her and take his rightful place as King now his father had disappeared.

The two men stopped near Babka's hiding-place. To her horror she heard them making plans to cut down the trees so that the timber could be sold.

When at last the men rode on Babka crept out of her hiding-place and went slowly back home. The forest was to be destroyed, and she and her friends the birds would be driven away. For how could she stay with the forest made hideous with the crash of falling trees, the noise of the woodcutters and all the devastation they would bring with them?

She was so distressed that she sat brooding by the hearth forgetful of everything else, until the cold made her get up to mend the fire and fill her apron with scraps for the waiting birds. Instead of smiling at them when they flocked around her she stood with tears pouring down her

cheeks. 'My poor little ones,' she whispered. 'What will happen to you when the trees are cut down?'

She was about to go in when she noticed what looked like a heap of feathers under the tree. Some poor bird had fallen exhausted with hunger, she thought, but a large bird, much larger than those that usually came to her bird-table. She gathered the limp creature tenderly in her apron and hurried in to the fire. The bird, though the size of a crow, was as light as a sparrow; she marvelled it could weigh so little as she gazed at its feathers of crimson and yellow. It must be a stranger driven off course by the autumn gales, for she had never seen such a bird before.

Its eyes were closed, but she could feel the fluttering of its heart, and its hawk-like beak kept opening and shutting as it gasped for breath. She set it down on the warm hearth. Above the fire a pot was simmering. It held her dinner: vegetable soup flavoured with dried mushrooms and thickened with a handful of meal.

She filled a spoon with the warm soup and let it trickle into the bird's open beak. It swallowed and then made a small sound as if asking for more.

'So you like it?' Babka said, and filled the spoon again.

The bird lifted its head as if the food and warmth had already given it strength. Babka chuckled and spoke to it lovingly.

With each spoonful it swallowed the bird became more alert. She could feel the warmth coming back to its body. Its eyes were open wide now, watching her without fear and with a strange glowing intensity. They were large and round, pale gold ringed with black. And all the time its beak was open asking for more.

'You need it more than I do, poor bird,' whispered Babka, as she spooned the last drop from the pot into its beak.

'There, it's all gone. You must be content.'

Babka had been so busy feeding the bird that she had not noticed the change which had come over its plumage. Now, as she put the spoon into the empty pot, her visitor rose to his feet and stood with the firelight gleaming on gold and crimson feathers. Life and lustre had flowed back to them and, as Babka watched, amazed at the sight, the bird seemed to grow larger and more magnificent. His tail, once a bunch of bedraggled feathers, was spread like a fan of gold, or like the sails of a proud ship in the flaming of sunset. On his head was a crest of filmy feathers, and his smooth sides and throat were of a pale burnished gold as sleek as silk. His radiance filled the small dark hut with a glow of golden light.

Babka knew that here was the very king of birds. She felt very humble as she knelt by the hearth, hardly able to believe that this was the poor dying creature she had rescued from the cold.

'Your Excellency,' she said shyly, and bowed her head.

'Because of your goodness I give you three wishes. Ask anything you will and it shall be granted,' said the bird, the light scintillating from his feathers as he strutted up and down.

In a flash Babka remembered the two men and their talk of cutting down the trees of the forest. She had forgotten her distress attending to the Golden Bird.

'I want the forest to stay just as it is, so that the birds and I won't be driven away,' she said.

The bird nodded gravely. 'It shall be granted. Your second wish, quickly?'

Babka looked about her. She might ask for another pot of soup, for it was the only thing she needed at the moment, but she was too well-mannered to remind her guest that he had eaten her supper. She could think of nothing else she wanted.

She went to the window hoping something might come into her mind, for the Golden Bird was clucking impatiently. She saw the birds about the water-hole and remembered how often in the winter she had to thaw out the ice with hot stones from her hearth so that they could drink.

'The water-hole! A little warm spring to bubble out of it that will never freeze,' she said.

'It shall be done,' replied the Golden Bird majestically. Now something for yourself. Your last wish. Quickly, for I must be gone.'

Fearful of offending him, Babka thought hard. Then she noticed that the fire needed attention. Her woodpile was low and the day was nearly over.

'A fire! A fire!' she cried triumphantly. 'A fire that will never go out.'

The bird shook his feathers until the room was aglow with ripples of light – gold, orange and red.

'An excellent wish, Babka. I have proved what I came to discover. That you are as wise as you are good. I acted the part of a dying bird to test you. If you are ever in trouble call on me and I will come. But it must be only in extremity, for I never answer twice. And let me give you a warning. The Queen is your enemy as well as mine.'

Then with a swift dancing movement and before Babka could thank him he went towards the fire. It flared up, blinding her by a rush of light, and when at last she could see again the bird had vanished.

She went to the door hoping to see him in the sky, but he had gone. The little birds were playing about the water-hole where a tiny spout of water splashed like a miniature fountain. Babka smiled at them and turned to the fire. Its heart burned with a steady glow, with the flames leaping about half-burned logs which, though they were on fire, never grew less. It had not been a dream.

Some moments later she was roused by the sound of horses and the loud voices of the two men she had seen earlier that day in the forest. Her door opened and the men came in.

'We are going to sit by your fire, mother, and warm ourselves,' said one of them.

Babka curtsied. She did not expect them to ask permission, for these were important men wearing the Queen's livery who must be treated with respect. The other man was taking packages from a saddlebag he had brought with him. He put a loaf of bread, butter, cheese, ham and a bottle of wine on the table.

'We'll eat here and thaw some of the chill out of our bones,' he said. 'Plates, old woman, and cups for our wine.'

Babka brought them clean napkins, plates and two wooden cups. Then she sat quietly in the corner while the men ate and drank. She was roused from her thoughts by a remark about the forest.

'No,' the younger man was saying. 'I've decided not to cut down the trees after all. It's too far from the river and it will cost too much to carry the timber by road.'

'But the Queen ordered –' began his companion, but the young man interrupted him.

'My mind is made up. The Queen will have to get her money from the woods nearer the river. There'll not be enough profit in this area to please her. We'd better be off if we want to get back before midnight.'

'That's a fine fire, mother. It's lucky for you you're burning dead wood. You know what happens to those who cut down new wood?' he said roughly.

'We've left you your supper,' added the other man, pointing to the remains of the food on the table.

Babka curtsied and went to the door to see them ride away. The birds had gone to roost and it was very quiet in the forest. Only the fountain played silently, and inside the hut danced the bright flame of the fire that would not go out. (Her three wishes had been granted.) Yet Babka was troubled. Why had the Golden Bird warned her that the Queen was her enemy? Why should she hate a poor old broom-maker living alone in the forest? What did the future hold? For if the Queen was a witch then she could see into the future, and it could only be in the days to come that danger would threaten.

Chapter Two

The Nut Maiden

Babka always knew when it was time for her to go gathering sweet chestnuts. When the first frosts of winter loosened the stalks so that the nuts tumbled to the ground Babka took her basket and set off into the heart of the forest. Babka was very fond of chestnuts, and it was not every year they ripened well. But it had been a long warm summer and she knew this would be a good year for them. She would be able to have boiled chestnuts, roasted chestnuts, and some she would bake and pound into flour and make little chestnut cakes for her friends in the village.

The chestnut trees grew in a lonely part of the forest several miles away from Babka's little house. They were tall towering trees standing alone in a grassy clearing, and there was always a special stillness in this spot which Babka loved.

As she had hoped, the nuts were very fine this year. Babka soon filled her basket and sat down to rest before returning home. Then she noticed, half hidden in the grass at her feet, the largest chestnut case she had ever seen. It was a round shaggy ball of the most delicate green, so large that when she made a cup of her hands they were only just big enough to hold it. She turned it round and round wonderingly. She shook it gently but it did not rattle. There must be some fine nuts inside, she told herself, but she did not break it open.

Instead she took off her kerchief and placed the ball carefully in it, tying up the corners to carry it more easily, and set off home. When she arrived there she laid the green shaggy ball in a basket of hay and placed it in the warm chimney-corner.

Every morning when she got up Babka looked at her treasure, and every evening when she went to bed. She would turn it round and round, examining it carefully, and after a few days she could see ridges in the skin where the case would eventually split open and spill out the ripe nuts.

One evening when she returned from the village laden with a little sack of provisions to last her through the winter Babka went as usual to look in the basket. The ball had split into many sections, showing a creamy whiteness within. It might have been a wide-petalled exotic flower. It was empty. Babka looked around. Where were the nuts? And then she saw in the dim corner of the hut a young girl watching her, startled and afraid. She had a skin as creamy white as a nut, long hair of rich chestnut brown and large dark eyes. She was the loveliest creature Babka had ever seen.

'I'm pleased to see you, my child,' she said gently. 'You are very welcome.'

The nut maiden smiled.

'Where have you come from?' Babka asked.

The girl shook her head.

'Can I stay with you?' she asked. 'I like it here.'

'As long as you wish,' replied Babka. 'Come and sit by the fire.'

So the nut maiden stayed with Babka in the forest and Babka named her Wanda. She taught her to milk the goats and feed the hens, but she would not let her make brooms, for that would have spoiled her pretty white hands.

Wanda was a merry girl. When Babka sat making her

brooms the nut maiden would sing to her, or dance about the room as lightly as a leaf in a breeze, twirling her green skirts and making her long plaits of hair swing out behind her. She grew tall and straight and prettier every day. Babka loved her dearly and worked harder than ever so that she could buy honey cakes, ribbons and pretty red shoes for her nut maiden.

Usually Wanda was obedient and docile, but sometimes she would wander alone in the forest all day until dusk fell. This made Babka very anxious, but she never reproached her. She knew she would lose her if she did. Wanda was a creature of the wild and Babka never wanted to tame a wild creature.

When the winter was over and Babka had to leave her and go to the village she would say: 'Do not go far from the hut while I'm away. If the woodcutters pass by go in and shut the door.'

But often when Babka returned Wanda would have forgotten her duties, and the goats were bleating to be milked, the hens cackling for food and there was no sign of the nut maiden. The gossips of the village whispered about Wanda among themselves. Foresters coming through the woods in the dusk told how they had seen her dancing alone, flitting about like a creature of another world, and when they had chased her she had fled, or suddenly disappeared, or changed into a tree, or led them astray in the loneliest parts of the forest. There were some who said Babka was a witch and the girl a creature she had made out of magic, but the more sensible villagers said Wanda was a gypsy girl whom Babka, with her kind heart, had taken in out of pity, for it was plain the girl was too delicate for the hard work most village girls had to do. They also murmured that Babka would be sorry she had given Wanda a home. No good would come of it, they said, shaking their heads.

Then it began to be whispered that Prince Stephen, the Queen's only son, was spending the days searching the forest for a beautiful maiden he had glimpsed sitting with a fawn at her feet among the chestnut trees. One of the Prince's grooms, whose parents lived in the village, told the story of how this maiden, too beautiful to be human, had fled at the sight of the hunters. She had disappeared into a thorn brake with a scream of fear, scattering the flowers she had gathered, and leaving behind a pair of little red shoes. The Prince had pursued the maiden on foot and ordered his groom to wait with the hounds and the horses. He had waited until dark when the Prince had appeared limping with tiredness, the little red shoes still in his hand. After this the Prince took to hunting alone.

Babka met the Prince for the first time one evening as she was feeding her birds before they went to roost. She saw a tired, handsome, bedraggled young man leading a white horse enter the clearing where her little house stood. She knew he was important by the silver buckles on his cloak, his jewelled embroidered gauntlets and the eagle's feather in his cap. His horse looked as tired as himself.

Babka curtsied low. 'Good evening, your Excellency,' she said in her quiet, timid voice.

'Have you seen a beautiful young girl pass this way?' he asked. 'She was wearing a green dress and had long brown hair and bare feet.'

'What would a gentleman want with a poor broom-maker's child?' Babka replied.

'So she lives here! Take me to her at once,' ordered the Prince sharply.

'She is not here. She's never been out quite so late before. Have you seen her in the forest?'

'A glimpse of her dancing under the chestnut trees miles from here. It's always the same. I search for hours and then

I see her, but she always runs away before I can catch her. I thought she came in this direction ... perhaps it was only the wind in the bushes or the bending of a young sapling. For she moves more lightly than a fawn and swifter than a squirrel.' The Prince sighed. 'I can think of nothing else,' he said.

He looked so baffled and unhappy that Babka was sorry for him despite her anxiety about Wanda.

'If your Excellency will please step inside. Wanda will not come while you are here. I will tell you what I can.'

Tying his horse to the tree-stump the Prince entered the hut and sat down on a stool.

'This girl ... who is she? Your grand-daughter or some spirit that you conjure up to mock travellers so that they lose their wits?' he said roughly. 'I'll get to the bottom of this mystery, old mother, if I have to hang you.'

Babka showed no fear at his words. She knew he was tormented with longing for Wanda.

'She is Wanda, a nut maiden. No fit companion for your Excellency. I have tried to teach her to behave like a village girl, but it is like teaching a bird. She is only happy here in the forest where I can watch over her. Forget her and go away. She can only bring you sorrow.'

Babka paused, waiting for the storm of anger she expected because she had spoken so freely, but the Prince's mood had changed to sadness. He had forgotten he was a Prince, heir to the country of the wide forests, he had forgotten his princely duties and the palace in the city on the hill. All he wanted was Wanda, the nut maiden.

'I can't forget her. Every night I lie in bed waiting until morning so that I can ride out and look for her in the forest. See! I must give her her shoes. She left them behind the first time I frightened her.'

'What will you do when you find her?' asked Babka.

'She shall have everything in the world. Jewels, furs, a palace of marble, horses to ride and servants to wait upon her. One day I shall make her a Queen, and every day she shall dance for me.'

Babka shook her head.

'If you were to shut her up in a great palace she would pine away. She must be free.'

'What do you advise, old mother?' asked the Prince humbly; he had forgotten he was talking to an old peasant woman, and only knew he could trust her wisdom and kindness.

'Give her a little house in the palace grounds away from the court where she can live among the trees and be as free as any wild creature of the forest. Tame her with patience and gentleness.'

'If I do this will you help me? I can make you rich. You can have everything you want.'

'I have all I need here in the forest,' replied Babka gravely.

And to his surprise the Prince believed her. In his search for Wanda he had strayed into a world unknown to courtiers and courts, a world where riches counted for little.

Babka knew that the Prince would never give up the nut maiden. If she refused to help him he would find others who might try to take her by force. Already the village was beginning to talk about the girl as if she were a witch. In a bad mood they might come hunting her themselves. It was better the Prince should protect Wanda, for Babka knew he loved her dearly.

'I will do what I can,' she promised him.

Chapter Three

The Nut Maiden
and the Prince

The Prince built Wanda a little house in the corner of the great park which surrounded the palace. There was a grove of chestnut trees near by and the paths which led to the house were arranged like a maze; only those who knew the secret could find the way to it. In front of the house was a deep pool fringed with willows and fed by a clear running stream. Wanda's mirror, he called it. All around were the ancient trees of the park and grassy clearings where deer browsed. To keep away inquisitive people he had a high wall built enclosing this part of the park, and inside the wall he planted a deep thicket of wild rose bushes. There were all kinds of devices within to amuse the nut maiden, little rustic bridges over the stream, a waterfall, a summerhouse with a little bell-cote that rang a carillon and banks of the most beautiful flowers.

While the house was being built the Prince rode every day to Babka's hut and Wanda welcomed him and came to love him. When he asked her to come away with him she went willingly, riding in front of him on the white horse in a new green silk gown and a cloak lined with scarlet velvet. Babka was sad as she watched them go. She knew that Wanda would have few friends at court.

Village gossip told her that the Queen was very angry about Wanda and hated her. The Queen had wanted the Prince to marry a wealthy princess of a nearby country,

but the Prince had refused. Many hoped that at last he was shaking off the Queen's magic influence.

The mystery of Wanda's birth, the rumours of her wild dancing in the forest, all these things helped the story put out by the Queen that the Prince was bewitched by a tree-spirit, who would lead him away from his own people and send him mad. The court was divided about this, and there were many who thought that a tree-spirit for a Queen, when the time came for the Prince to inherit the kingdom, would be preferable to the present Queen, but they dare not utter their thoughts or show kindness to Wanda, for they feared the Queen's anger.

For a little while some of the villagers hinted that Babka had used the nut maiden for her own ends, but when they saw she still went on making her brooms and was as poor as ever they knew they had been foolish. It was not easy to believe that Babka, with her kindly ways, could be a witch.

Time went by. The Prince was still very much in love and spent nearly all his time at Wanda's retreat; and the court, it seemed, grumbled because they saw so little of him. But there was no other news and Babka began to think that her fears about the Queen harming Wanda had been unnecessary.

The autumn came again, and the beginning of winter. On the day of the first snow, as the sky was darkening and the first large flakes began to fall, Babka came back from selling her brooms carrying a little sack of meal to keep her through the long weeks when she would be cut off from the village.

This year she was not sorry to see the snow. She had her birds and her cheerful fire, which was like a welcoming friend, and she knew that however hard the winter she would be able to keep snug and warm. Since Wanda had left her Babka no longer enjoyed the gossip of the village.

There had been too many suspicious glances and malicious questions. Now she would be alone and at peace in the forest.

She was thinking of this as she trudged along, her head bent a little to keep the snow out of her eyes. It was not until she reached her door that she saw the white horse of the Prince tied to the tree-stump, its gleaming body ivory yellow against the pure whiteness of the snow.

Babka went quickly into the hut. The Prince was sitting by the fire, his head in his hands. He looked sad and very tired.

'What has happened?' asked Babka. 'Where is Wanda?'

'She is gone,' replied the Prince. 'I had to leave her for a few days ... it was an affair of state. I told her not to go far from the house while I was gone. But I was detained. It was a plot to get me out of the way. As soon as I had gone the Queen bribed one of my men to show her the way through the maze. The Queen then took Wanda away, pretending she wanted to teach her how to take her proper place in the palace. But she shut her in the old tower – my little wild maiden shut away from the woods and the free life she loved!'

The Prince groaned and put his head in his hands again.

'Where is she now?' asked Babka very gently.

The Prince raised his head.

'Gone! Gone! I hoped she was here.'

But one look at Babka's face told him his last hope was dead.

'One of my men I left to watch over Wanda rode after me as soon as the Queen took her away. It was several days before he could reach me. I rode back at once, without stopping to eat or sleep. The Queen did not expect me so soon and she was alarmed at my anger. I forced her to give me the key of the tower. She was afraid I would raise the

people of the city against her. When I opened the door of the room at the top of the tower where they had put Wanda it was empty.'

'She had escaped?' asked Babka.

'There was only a small window barred with iron. A bird could not have escaped from that room through the window, and the door had been guarded night and day. I questioned the guards. I know they were telling me the truth when they vowed Wanda had not escaped from the tower. Nevertheless I sent out search parties. But she has completely disappeared. On the bed I found this. . . .'

The Prince held out his hand. In it was a large round shaggy chestnut case like the one Babka had found in the forest under the chestnut trees. She took it gently, turning it round and round.

'Do you think she'll come back?' asked the Prince.

'Who can tell?' replied Babka, but there was no hope in her voice.

After the Prince had gone Babka sat deep in thought for a long time. Then she went to the woodshed and took out her spade. Near the door of the hut, in a spot where the first rays of the sun fell in the morning, she dug a small hole. The earth was soft under the snow and as she put her hand in it she felt it was still warm with the summer's sun. She placed the chestnut carefully in the hole, then covered it with earth. The snow was falling steadily now and in a few minutes the earth she had exposed was covered with a white carpet.

In the spring a strong green shoot appeared where Babka had buried the nut. She made a little fence of thorn twigs to protect it and every evening watered it carefully. Soon there were two green leaves on the shoot, and in a little while it had grown taller into a chestnut sapling, waving its leaves in every gentle breeze. Babka always bent to look at

it when she went in and out of the hut, and she fancied the soft green leaves waved to her as if in greeting.

As for the Prince, he set off on a long expedition in foreign lands to forget his sorrow and, some said, to find another bride.

Chapter Four

The Dwarf

One day when Babka was coming back from collecting herbs she met a dwarf. He was an ugly little creature with a hump on his back and his face puckered into lines of discontent and bad temper. His pale amber eyes looked out from under ragged eyebrows. He was dirty, his feet were wrapped in rags, and he wore a battered hat which was too small sitting on top of an unkempt mass of red hair sprouting in all directions. He walked with a side-ways crawl, as if he were perpetually looking over one shoulder ready to run if an enemy appeared.

'Good day,' said Babka in her small timid voice.

'Good day indeed! It's a bad day for me,' grumbled the dwarf. 'I've been chased from village to village, beaten with sticks and had fierce dogs set on me. You wouldn't say it was a good day if you were lost in this horrible forest with the trees putting out their roots to trip you and briars stretching out their thorns to scratch you, and if you hadn't had a mouthful of food all day.'

'The forest is my home. It never does those things to me,' replied Babka. 'But if you are hungry you can share my dinner.'

She sat down on a fallen tree-trunk and took a flat cake of bread, a bottle of goat's milk and a wooden cup from the big pocket of her apron. She broke the bread in half and poured some milk into the cup and offered them to him. He looked at her like a wild animal fearing a trap. Then, with a swift movement, he snatched the piece of bread and crammed it into his mouth, retreating as he did so as if he thought she would take it away again.

Babka paid no heed to him. She ate her own piece, throwing the crumbs to a robin who hopped about her feet.

'I could do with more,' muttered the dwarf as he put down the cup.

'Poor thing!' Babka said to herself. 'It's because he's tired and frightened that he's so uncouth and his speech so rough.'

'Can I set you on your way? Where are you going?' she asked.

'I've nowhere to go. Nobody wants me. I shall wander in the forest until I fall down and die of hunger.'

The dwarf looked at Babka with an artful expression, trying to see how far he could take advantage of her simplicity.

'I would make a good servant. I'm strong. I can draw water, chop wood, dig the garden, plant cabbage,' he went on, watching the look of pity on Babka's face.

'Why did you leave your last place?' she asked.

The dwarf was put out by this unexpected question.

'Because they jeered at me . . . mocked my hump. I couldn't stand it any longer,' he whined.

'But you must have done something to upset them,' persisted Babka.

'They said I stole the cream, put water in the churn so that the butter would not come. Everybody hates me because I'm ugly,' muttered the dwarf.

'I can't afford a servant. I live by making brooms. If you like to come and help in my garden I'll feed you and mend your clothes. Then you could find a better place,' suggested Babka.

She did not want this ill-mannered dwarf in her hut,

frightening the birds with his rough ways and scowling at her from under his bushy eyebrows, but she could not leave him to starve in the forest and it was plain he was unable to look after himself. She did not see the grin of satisfaction which flitted across the dwarf's face.

'I'll come,' he muttered ungraciously, and picked up her sack of herbs, shuffling behind her with his noisy, ungainly walk which made Babka feel quite uncomfortable, because she always walked quietly in the forest.

It did not take her long to discover her mistake. The dwarf was strong and worked hard. He cut poles for her brooms and helped in the garden, and this gave her more time to work and make extra money to buy food to keep him. But when his work was done he would sit watching her with an unpleasant scowl on his face. Nothing made him happy or contented. He was always following her about, asking questions and never satisfied she was speaking the truth. But Babka's life was so simple that he soon discovered she had nothing to hide, and this made him more miserable than ever.

The dwarf hated the birds. When he thought she was not looking he would frighten them from the water-hole and bird-table.

One day coming back earlier than usual from the village Babka caught him standing by the water-hole waving his arms and screaming with rage at the birds who flew around out of reach trying to get at the water. When he saw her he slunk away into the woodshed, muttering evilly.

Babka prepared the supper and called to him that it was ready. He came scowling, and sat down on his stool without a word of greeting.

'What were you doing at the water-hole?' she asked.

'The birds ... they mock me ... they're always mocking me,' he grumbled.

'You must leave them alone,' replied Babka sternly, for though she was a timid old woman she knew that if she did not hold her own this time the dwarf would become master in her little house. It was time to teach him a lesson. On the table was a dish of honey cakes. The dwarf was very fond of honey cakes, and as her brooms had sold well that day she had bought them as a treat for him.

'You would not let the birds drink, so they shall have your honey cakes,' she said, crumbling them quickly. She went to the door and threw the pieces to the waiting birds.

With a wild bellow of rage the dwarf rushed out, but the birds also liked honey cakes. They came down in a rush of wings, chattering excitedly as they picked up the pieces and flew off into the trees to eat them.

'I'll show you! I'll show you!' shouted the dwarf, dancing and stamping with rage.

He rushed to the shed and brought out a spade.

'They'll never drink here again. I'll fill up the water-hole,' he roared, and his harsh voice went echoing through the trees.

Babka stood at the door smiling a little as a small bird picked up a large crumb from under his feet and seemed to wave it in his face as it flew away. All Babka's fear of the dwarf had vanished and she felt quite serene.

'If you meddle with the water you'll be sorry. You can do nothing to stop it,' she said.

'Out of my way, old witch,' he shouted, pushing her roughly aside.

He started to throw great spadesful of earth into the water-hole, working in a frenzy of rage so that he seemed more like a giant than a dwarf, but, even so, Babka was not afraid of him. She knew the Golden Bird would not tolerate any interference with one of his gifts.

The hole was soon filled up, but the dwarf could not stop

the flow of water. It pushed its way through the earth, flinging high jets of muddy water which sprayed out and soaked him. It leapt and swayed in his direction as if guessing every movement he must make, the jets leaning this way and that as he tried to avoid them.

The gentle fountain, once only a few inches high, had turned into a waterspout, towering into the sky and then falling on the dwarf's head and shoulders so that he staggered under its weight. The harder he worked the fiercer fell the water. He was soon drenched to the skin. His shaggy hair was plastered to his head and water dripped from his ears and face and from all parts of him.

Babka watched in amazement, while the small birds flew from the trees and perched on her arms and shoulders. A particularly vicious jet of water caught the dwarf full in the eyes, blinding him so that he staggered and slipped, falling face downward on the huge pile of earth he had placed over the water-hole. For a moment he lay still, then with a roar of terror he got up, threw down the spade, and rushed away into the forest, leaving a long trail of water as he ran.

The following morning when Babka opened the door of the hut the water-hole, with its little fountain playing, looked as if nothing had happened.

The next time Babka went to the village she asked the villagers if they had seen the dwarf.

'He's gone back to the Queen,' said Norbert, the cripple, who spent most of his days on a bench outside the inn minding everybody's business.

'Was he one of the Queen's dwarfs?' asked Babka in surprise. 'He never spoke about the Queen or the palace.'

Norbert sniffed. 'He didn't want you to know. I suppose he told you he ran away from a farm where they ill-treated him?'

'Yes, he did,' said Babka.

Norbert sniffed again. 'He came to the inn as wet as a dog that had been thrown in the river, threw away his sodden rags, bought new clothes, had a meal with wine and chicken and then went off on one of the landlord's horses. And paid for all these things with a gold piece. You didn't pay him for his work with gold pieces, did you, Babka?' laughed the cripple.

The villagers who had gathered round laughed also, knowing how poor she was.

'But how do you know he was one of the Queen's dwarfs?' Babka questioned.

'Where else would he get gold pieces except at court?' replied Norbert testily. 'And I remember seeing him, or one like him, in the Queen's livery when she was hunting in the forest last year. He was perched on a very high horse, with a jester's cap on his head, and lashing out with his whip when the children laughed at him, the ugly little toad. He was up to no good, Babka. He had some reason for hiding at your place, and I'd like to know what it was.'

'So would I,' replied Babka uneasily. 'But I'm very glad he's gone.'

Why should the Queen have sent the dwarf to spy on her? Had she heard of the magic fountain and the magic fire and sent the dwarf to see if they really existed? Babka had never spoken of the gifts of the Golden Bird to anyone. But then the Queen had magical powers. She might have discovered these things for herself and sent the dwarf to make certain about them. Babka puzzled over the mystery for some days, but as the dwarf did not reappear and life went on as quietly as usual it soon ceased to trouble her.

Chapter Five

Bat-Ears, the Robber

One evening as Babka was on her way home from the village she saw coming towards her a young man driving a cow. It was Joseph, the son of a farmer in the village, a frank, jolly young man, kind to his animals and always willing to help anyone less fortunate than himself. Babka had watched him grow up and she was very fond of him.

But now he looked tired and dejected, and to her surprise he was flicking the cow with his stick. Not that the cow seemed afraid of him. He had always treated her kindly so she refused to take his bad temper seriously.

'Why, Joseph, what has the poor beast done?' asked Babka. 'Let us sit in the sun for a while and you can tell me your news.' And Babka sat down by the wayside.

'You look very contented, Babka,' Joseph replied enviously.

'It's a fine evening. The spring has come. What is troubling you, Joseph?' Babka asked.

Joseph sighed.

'It's Anna. I want to marry her, but her miserly old stepfather refuses to give her a dowry and my father refuses to let me marry without one. "Find a girl with a good dowry and I'll set you up in a farm of your own by the river," he said to me this morning. Think of it, Babka, a farm of my own! And I can't have it because Anna's stepfather won't give her a dowry. He's a rich man, but he's mean. He'll

not let Anna go because she works as hard as two women.'

'There are other girls with dowries who would be pleased to have you, Joseph,' replied Babka mildly.

'I want Anna. I'm promised to Anna. If I can't have her I'll go to the city and join the Prince's bodyguard. Or I'll go and seek Bat-Ears, the robber. He's been seen this side of the river. There's a good reward for whoever captures him, as much as a dowry. They say he's a terrible man, as fierce as a hungry bear and stronger than a lion. Perhaps he'll fight and kill me and that will be the end of it. That's what I'll do. As soon as I've taken the cow to her pasture I'll go looking for Bat-Ears.'

Babka rose and shook out her skirts.

'Don't despair, Joseph,' she said comfortingly. 'Do nothing until tomorrow. I'll think of some way to help you if I can. Come and see me early in the morning on your way to the milking. Don't do anything tonight, will you?'

Joseph agreed to wait until the next day. 'You're clever, Babka. You can help me if anyone can,' he replied, and went on his way looking less miserable.

'At least he'll do nothing rash tonight,' Babka told herself. 'In the morning he'll not be so angry and then the idea of leaving home won't appeal to him.' For she knew Joseph loved his home and his cattle and would never be happy anywhere else.

It was growing dark by the time she arrived at her little house. She fed the hens and milked her goats, and was just ladling out the soup from the pot over the fire when the door opened and she saw filling the doorway the largest man she had ever seen in her life, and the ugliest.

He was wide as well as tall and his bulky clothes made him larger than life-size. He wore a furry cloak over his shoulders and carried a thick club in his hand. A wide leather belt round his waist was ornamented with large brass studs, and in it he carried several fierce-looking weapons, including two pistols, a long thin knife in a sheath, a two-edged dagger and various other implements which could be used for anything from cracking a nut to digging a grave. Red leather riding-boots came up to his knees and they were trimmed with silver cords and tassels.

His round face was a mottled purplish colour and he had a shaggy beard and moustache out of which his lips looked very red and greedy. There was more hair on his face than on his head, for he was nearly bald except for a fringe of dirty grey curls at the neck. His large crumpled ears stood out like jug handles. Babka knew at once that he was Bat-Ears, the robber. No wonder the women in the district had been terrified by the rumour that he had been seen in the forest. Babka hid her alarm, however, and smiled at him timidly.

'Won't you come in and sit down?' she asked mildly, because she knew he meant to come in anyway.

'Why don't you scream, old woman?' shouted the robber, his voice like the roar of an angry bull.

Babka would have been frightened if it had not occurred to her that it was rather absurd of him to make such a noise to frighten an old woman who had no strength to resist him.

'What good would it do?' she replied with a shrug of her shoulders.

Fetching another bowl she filled it with soup and put it on the table. Bat-Ears shut the door, secured it with the bar and then strode to the hearth and stood warming himself.

'That's a fine fire you have, mother. I'll be cosy and snug here,' he said with the lordly air of one taking possession.

'You can stay if you wish. I shall not harm you,' replied Babka mildly.

Bat-Ears laughed until the tears rolled down his cheeks.

'You'll not harm me! That's good,' he shouted.

He took off his heavy belt with its assortment of weapons and threw it on the floor with a great clatter.

'Onion soup? It smells good but I want meat, old woman. Good red meat and good red wine.'

'This is all I have,' said Babka, and began to drink her soup.

'How can I fight and kill and rob without meat? A fowl! Two fowls! I heard them cackling when I came in. I'll wring their necks and you shall pluck them and then roast them by this splendid fire.'

Babka went on with her soup and made no reply.

'I'd wring your neck and roast you instead, but you'd be too skinny and tough. Come on, old woman. Out with you and fetch the birds. I'd better come with you. For you might run off and bring help and then I'd have to cut your throat before I had my supper.'

Babka finished the last spoonful of soup and then slipped quickly out to the fowl-house with Bat-Ears blundering after her. The birds were on their perches and, opening the door as widely as she could, she began to drive them out, pretending to catch them but making such a commotion that it was difficult to tell what she was doing. Bat-Ears cursed in the darkness as the birds escaped to the trees.

'Catch them,' he shouted, stamping with rage.

'You've frightened them with your shouting,' Babka grumbled, and catching up an old broom she pushed the twiggy head into Bat-Ears's face, blinding him for a moment.

'Oh dear! There isn't room in the fowl-house for two of us. You're so big and clumsy,' she scolded, as she gave the last hen a push out of the door.

Only the cock was left, and he, to protect his hens, became fighting mad and attacked the robber fiercely.

'Catch that cock!' ordered Bat-Ears, the blood streaming

down his cheek from a vicious thrust of the bird's claws.

'I've got him,' replied Babka, and caught the cock in her arms and then, with a reassuring shake, she threw him out of the door and heard him fly into the trees.

'Why didn't you help me?' she said to Bat-Ears, who was wiping the blood from his face. 'Now they have all gone. We'll never catch them tonight unless you can climb trees in the dark. Let's go back to the hut or your soup will be cold.'

Bat-Ears followed her, grumbling and whining.

'I'll shoot the lot of them. Wait till I get my pistols.'

'If you do, the charcoal burners in the forest will hear the shots and come and see what is happening. They're strong fierce men, not frightened like the villagers.'

'Then we'd better go back to the hut,' said the robber, pushing Babka before him. 'And you'd better bring out all the food you've got because I'm starving, and when I'm hungry I'm very terrible.'

But Babka was no longer afraid of him. She had seen how frightened he had been when the cock attacked him. He is stupid as well as a coward, she told herself, as she pretended to search her cupboard. But all she brought out was a plate of stale porridge, half a loaf and a piece of goat's cheese.

Bat-Ears swallowed the porridge and cheese, finished the loaf to the last crumb and scraped out the soup pot. Then he took off his boots, unbuttoned his jacket and looked at Babka sitting placidly in the chimney-corner.

'I'll rest for a few hours. I must be on my way before dawn. They're searching for me, but they will do nothing in the dark and by daylight I'll be far away. You think you'll tell them which way I've gone, don't you, old woman?' he asked with an ugly grin.

'What else can I do if they ask me?' replied Babka.

'Well, I'll tell you. You won't be able to say anything. Before I go I'll cut your throat with my sharp knife!'

'Will you grant me one wish before I die?' Babka asked. 'I'm old and have few pleasures. One is my fire. I love to watch the wood burn until only the glowing embers remain. Let me do this through one more night. That's all I ask '

'You think I'll fall asleep and you'll make up the fire,' he sneered.

'There's no wood in the hut and you've bolted the door,' replied Babka mildly.

'Then you shall have your wish. When the fire has died down to a few smouldering embers you die. Until then let's enjoy ourselves. We'll play cards. It will keep me awake and I can watch you don't make up the fire.'

Bat-Ears took a pack of cards from his wallet and explained the game. 'Bring out your money, old woman,' he shouted boisterously.

'I'm a poor broom-maker. I have no money. You must lend me some.'

'But no!' replied Bat-Ears. 'You might win more than you borrowed.'

'It will be all yours in the morning,' said Babka, and she thought again what a very stupid man he was.

They started to play and it did not take Babka long to discover the cards were marked and that Bat-Ears was cheating. After a while she began to win and this annoyed him very much. It was her purpose to keep him playing as long as possible, so she began to let him win a little, for she knew he would not cut her throat until he had won all the money. If she could keep him playing until dawn Joseph would come and capture him.

Babka was very weary and her eyes longed for sleep. She glanced at the fire. It burned brightly, its flames lighting up the room and making it very warm. She gazed at it dreamily, forgetting the game for a moment, and Bat-Ears threw down his cards and picked up the coins on the table.

'I've won, old woman! I've won! You thought you could beat me, but nobody can beat Bat-Ears!'

He looked at the fire with a puzzled expression on his great round face.

'Your fire burns very slowly,' he muttered. 'Well, I promised you should see it die down and so you shall. I'll take a nap. If you move I shall hear you. I'm not called Bat-Ears for nothing. If a mouse stirs I hear it, asleep or awake.'

Folding his arms he let his chin sink on his chest and closed his eyes. Babka sat very still. How much longer till dawn, she wondered? How much longer? She sat there watching the leaping flames, and it seemed to her that the glowing heart of the fire was shaped like the Golden Bird, luminous and wonderful. She was comforted and shut her eyes to rest them, but not to sleep, for she was listening all the time.

The robber awoke with a start. He looked at Babka on her stool with her eyes closed, her face serene.

'Did you hear anything, old woman?' he shouted.

'You were dreaming,' Babka replied. But she knew that he, also, had heard the faint crowing of a cock in the distance.

Although no light came through the shuttered window of the hut, outside in the eastern sky the dawn must be breaking. On the hearth the flames rose higher as if to welcome the morning.

'You've mended the fire while I slept,' he said angrily.

'You know I haven't touched it,' replied Babka boldly.

The robber looked around uneasily.

'You're a witch. You've put a spell on me and now morning is here when I should be far away. They burn witches.'

the room, and looking it over again. He gazed at it once, this together, the game. For a moment, and her question:

"I'm an old world for you? You thought you really

"But me, technology can tear from its...

little back down and lie a little, I would stand up and look at his performing it.

You can sit quite now to see how to get up and fall into sleep. You have smiled near you, I must... called Barbara fire walking. It was true at first and it was a great deal of closing pictures, he let the face and say, be quiet and she had lingered, it was so very still. There was a longer till then, she wandered. She went longer than before

her and into her surrounding old woman who showed

You were dreaming. Barbara said for she knew that she sat quiet and been staring down ahead and laid into the distance.

And then it came from the shuttered window, he had given it and came into the house he could open all the doors to welcome...

He came towards her with his arms outstretched and lifted her as if she were a doll. He was about to put her on the fire when leaping flames and smoke came out into the room as if blown by a great wind, flames and smoke shaped like a monstrous bird with angry beating wings. It came closing round his chest and beard, burning and choking him so that he dropped Babka in a panic. Blinded by the smoke he dashed round the room screaming with pain and fright, overturning the stools and knocking himself against the heavy table. Babka ran after him trying to put out the flames with her apron. She was unhurt. The fire had not touched her.

'Roll on the floor,' she commanded.

The terrified Bat-Ears rolled on the floor, while Babka buffeted him soundly with one of her brooms until the flames were beaten out. He was a miserable sight as he lay on the floor, his face blackened, his clothes burned and his beard singed. He was quite unnerved. Great tears rolled down his dirty cheeks making white streaks in the grime.

'I didn't mean to harm you. It was a joke. Take my money-bag. Take my knives. Take everything I've got!' he cried.

Babka unbarred the door. She could hear Joseph whistling as he came towards the hut. In a few seconds he had Bat-Ears safely trussed up with his own belt and Babka's clothes-line.

'Now you can claim the reward and use it for Anna's dowry,' said Babka smiling.

Joseph was bewildered by the suddenness of it all.

'You came just in time to save me. Off you go and take him away,' Babka said briskly.

And Joseph, still looking surprised but very happy, led the miserable Bat-Ears away. 'Thank you, Babka,' he said, 'I shall never forget what you have done.'

Babka began to make everything neat again. On the floor where it had fallen during his mad rush round the room was the robber's money-bag. She looked at it thoughtfully for a moment, then picked it up and hid it in the loft under a sack of potatoes.

'One day it might be useful,' she said to herself.

Chapter Six

Babka and the Magician

The Queen's magician lived at the top of the old tower in the palace grounds. Here, like a spider in a hole, he spent his days weaving spells, mixing potions, stirring his brews over a strange fire of blue and green flames. The damp stone walls were hung with mildewed black draperies, and the dried skins of bat and bird, toad and salamander, bundles of herbs and roots filled the dusty shelves.

He wore a tattered robe ornamented with stars and crescents out of which his long skinny arms and pointed fingers poked like the twigs of a dead tree, and his head, under a velvet skull cap, was yellow as old ivory and smooth as an egg. His face was nothing but a high, bony forehead, a sharp beaky nose and sharper chin, with burning dark eyes glowing like lamps within his skull. For more years than he could remember he had been trying to turn base metals into gold, but though the Queen loved gold more than anything else in the world all her magic and his arts could not produce it.

Now his fire was out and his crucibles were empty. He had come to the end of his spells. Lumps of grey lead, phials of yellow and blue powder lay neglected on the heavy table. The only clean object in his room was a large crystal ball, white and shining, into which he gazed hour after hour, trying to find some way of making gold to satisfy the Queen. She had said that if he did not do so in the next few days he must die. The Queen had said this before, but the magician knew that this time she meant it.

He had tried everything. In one last despairing effort he took up his crystal; there was nothing else left to do.

For hours he sat motionless. Then he saw within the ball a little old woman sitting by the fire in a hut in the forest making brooms. The picture faded and he knew it would not come again. Grasping his tall staff to support his tottering steps the magician rose and went to the door and called his servant Janek, who came running.

'Yes, master?' said Janek.

'Do you know a broom-maker who lives in the forest?'

'There's Babka. Some say she's a witch, for when she calls the birds they come to her, and some say she's just a crazy old woman,' replied Janek.

The magician clutched the boy's ear with fingers like talons so that he squirmed with pain.

'Fetch me a mule to ride, and lead me there,' he commanded.

'It's a long way, master.'

'If we're not there by nightfall I'll turn you into a mouse and myself into an owl – a hunting owl,' threatened the magician, as the boy ran to fetch the mule.

A full moon was rising as the magician on a mule, led by the footsore Janek, turned into the clearing by Babka's little house. They could see a flicker of light from her fire shining from the window. The forest was ghostly in the moonlight and it was very still.

'There's the hut, master,' said Janek, helping his master down from the mule.

'My things,' snapped the magician. 'Then take the mule and go. I will send for you when I'm ready. I have secret business with Babka. Tell nobody where I've gone.'

'No, master,' said Janek, and swinging himself into the

saddle he rode off as fast as he could, while the magician gathered his robes together and tottered to the hut.

Babka smiled almost as if she were expecting him.

'Come in,' she said. 'The soup is ready.'

The magician, after a solemn greeting, sat down and took the bowl of soup she offered.

'They can't make soup in the palace kitchens as good as this,' he said. 'Unless you help me it may be my last bowl of soup.'

'How can I help you?' asked Babka wonderingly. 'I am only a poor broom-maker.'

The magician took his crystal and turned it in his hands. The light from the fire was reflected in its depth, but nothing else appeared. He looked at Babka despairingly.

'Unless you help me I must die, for the Queen is very angry with me. I've slaved for years trying to turn base metals into gold. Will you look into the crystal? Can you see gold in it?'

'Your gold and mine are not the same,' Babka answered, but she took the crystal and looked into it.

'What did you see?' asked the magician eagerly, when she put it down.

'The sunflowers in my garden like a host of suns, with hearts of red, gold and yellow petals for the pointed rays,' she replied.

'I knew you could help me,' cried the magician excitedly. 'Tomorrow at dawn you must give them to me.'

Babka could not believe that her sunflowers could possibly help the magician to make gold, but she was too kind-hearted to refuse him.

As soon as it was light next day they went out into the garden to gather them. They did not look golden in the cool morning light but a dingy yellow, heavy with dew. The magician looked at them gloomily, as if he also had his doubts, but fumbling in his robes he took his silver scissors from the chain about his waist and cut off the flower heads.

'What shall I do without my sunflower seeds in the winter?' Babka said.

'If you've read the crystal rightly I'll give you a sack, a dozen sacks, of seeds when I've made gold,' replied the magician.

Babka did not believe in his kind of magic and she was certain he would be disappointed again, but it was useless to tell him this; but she grieved for her sunflowers. They made her little garden so gay, and the seeds helped to feed the birds in bad weather.

All day long the magician toiled over the fire stirring a rank-smelling mixture in his pot, but no gold appeared. Babka, seeing he was faint with exhaustion, took the pot off the fire and placed it outside while she prepared a meal.

'It's time to rest and eat,' she said firmly.

When they had eaten and rested the magician said appealingly :

'When I looked in the crystal I saw you in this hut. You are the only one who can save me from the wrath of the Queen. Look into the crystal again. Think about gold.'

Babka took the ball into her hands, turning it slowly round and round. She thought of gold, all the golden things she had ever known, and slowly a picture formed in the heart of the crystal and she saw the jet of water rising from the water-hole, then falling in a silver shower. The silver changed to gold, liquid gold, and she knew the water had caught the glancing rays of the sun as it did for a few moments at a certain time each evening when the sky was clear. The gold faded and the water became silver again, and then the picture vanished altogether.

Babka gave a sigh and put the ball down on the table.

'What did you see? What did you see?' demanded the magician, his eyes gleaming hungrily.

When she told him he cried out:

'A drop of the magic water, gathered at the moment the sun turns it into liquid gold! At last after all these years I've discovered the secret!'

'The water-hole was made for the birds. It has nothing to do with the gold you want to make,' said Babka firmly.

And she was right. When evening came and the setting sun turned the silver water to gold the magician put a few drops in his crucible and began his work. The golden colour vanished from the water as soon as he touched it and never appeared again. The result was as disappointing as before.

Shaking with tiredness the magician sank down on the floor. Babka looked at him with pity and went to the door to let out the horrible smell of the magician's brew. In the distance she heard the sound of hoofs. Someone was riding towards the hut, urging the horse with whip and voice. It was Janek, the magician's red-headed servant.

'The Queen is coming! The Queen is coming!' he shouted. 'I've ridden hard to warn you. The executioner is with her. If you've not discovered how to make gold he will cut off your head. Quick, we must hide in the forest.'

The magician shook his head.

'I'm too old to run away. Wherever I hide the Queen will find me. I fear the Queen may wreak her vengeance on you, Babka, as well. You know the forest. Hide while there is still time.'

'No. I stay with you,' replied Babka. 'I have done no harm.'

'Look once more into the crystal, Babka,' urged Janek, for he was a good-hearted boy and wanted to help his master. He set the pot on the fire again.

Once more Babka took the crystal between her hands.

She saw the flickering fire, the hearth, her unfinished brooms reflected in its surface and then, in the very middle, appeared a vision of a sheep-skin bag tied with a leathern thong. It was the robber's money-bag filled with gold pieces which she had found after Joseph had captured Bat-Ears.

'Stir the pot! Stir the pot!' she cried to the boy and, climbing the ladder to the loft, she brought down the bag, untied the thong with trembling fingers and emptied the gold pieces into the pot.

'Burn, fire, burn!' she urged, and the flames leapt high.

It was so hot that they had to retreat from the hearth as the contents of the pot hissed and bubbled.

In the far distance they could hear the sound of galloping horses.

'The Queen!' muttered the magician, tucking his beard into his robe lest the flames caught it as he stirred the pot. 'This time she'll be satisfied. You have saved my life, Babka.''

'She'll want more gold, more and more, and that is all I have. What will you do next time?' asked Babka.

The magician smiled craftily.

'When she sees this gold she'll be hoping all the time I will do it again. My lost power will return. The Court will tremble when I chant my spells. You also have powerful charms. Come back with me to the palace. You shall have fine clothes and serving women, anything you want.'

'I have everything I want here in the forest. If you want to do me a service go away quickly and never mention my name, for the Queen is my enemy,' replied Babka.

'As you say. One day I may be able to repay you. I never forget a debt,' replied the magician.

Strength had returned to his shaking limbs. He stood in the doorway as the procession began to appear in the clearing, then he held up his wand commanding them to halt.

Meanwhile Janek had set out the moulds and was holding the pot ready to pour the liquid gold into them as soon as the Queen appeared.

Slowly he began to pour and a sigh of astonishment went up from the riders as they watched. With a flourish the executioner sheathed his great sword. The Queen motioned her attendants to fall back so that she could inspect the gold. Her baleful glance swept over the scene, at the triumphant magician, the red-headed youth and Babka curtseying respectfully. Her glance lingered for a moment on Babka, then her lip curled contemptuously.

'It is well. Your lives are spared. We'll return to the palace at once,' she said to the magician.

She jerked the jewelled bridle and her white palfrey tossed its head, setting the silver bells on its harness jingling.

'Let some of you look to the gold,' she commanded.

The leader of the escort, a handsome young captain in the Queen's uniform of green and silver, gave his orders briskly and the cavalcade moved away, leaving behind two soldiers to guard the cooling cold, and Janek to gather together his master's crucibles and instruments.

'Is it true you're a witch, old mother?' asked one of the soldiers.

'Why do you live so deep in the forest all alone?' asked the other one, who was gay and happy now the Queen had disappeared.

Babka smiled at them timidly. 'The magician came here because he wanted to get away where none could see how he made his gold,' she replied.

Janek, having tied his master's belongings to his horse's saddle, joined them. He looked at Babka with his sharp eyes. He had lost his fear of her and recognized her as a good friend. He was full of admiration for her generosity. He also wanted to ask her where she got the bag of gold, but that was impossible with the soldiers listening. He felt, however, he must give her a word of warning.

'The Queen eyed you strangely, Babka. It's well you live far from the palace,' he said.

'Hush! She'll hear you,' said the young soldier, looking round fearfully.

'Her ears are long and her eyes are everywhere,' said the other soldier. 'She is terrible. When she looks at me my bones turn to water, yet I have fought in battle and was never afraid of the enemy.'

When they had gone Babka went into the hut. The robber's empty bag was on the floor. One golden coin had escaped and lay twinkling beside it. She put it in the bag and returned it to its hiding-place.

She was behind with her work because of the time she had spent helping the magician, so she settled down to finish a batch of half-made brooms, thankful that peace had returned to the forest.

Chapter Seven

The Magician pays his Debt

A few days after Babka had helped the magician to make gold she was sitting by the door of her house tying her brooms. It was a bright morning and as she worked she watched a troop of redpolls and siskins bathing in the little fountain. It was a peaceful scene and Babka was content.

Then the birds rose with a shrill chatter of alarm and flew away into the tree-tops. Babka looked around. What had startled them? The shadow of a hawk, or were strangers near? Then from behind the hut on both sides stepped four men in the Queen's livery. They had silently surrounded the hut.

Babka was surprised she had not heard them coming. Why should these men approach so secretly as if they were hunting something or someone, she thought.

'Are you Babka, the broom-maker?' asked one who was in command.

Babka pointed to the pile of brooms at her feet.

'Do you want to buy some brooms?' she asked.

'It's you we want, not your brooms. Get up now and come with us,' he said roughly. 'You'd better take this as a sign of your trade.' And he thrust a broom into her hand.

'Where are you taking me?' asked Babka. But the man did not answer.

'First let me put on a clean apron.'

'Oh, no! You're not going into the hut, to disappear up

the chimney and make us look a pack of fools,' said one of the other men. 'Shall we tie her arms? We don't want her to escape.'

Babka looked at them in surprise.

'You are four strong men. Won't you look a little foolish tying up a poor old woman lest she run away from you?' she asked.

'You're a witch. Witches play tricks on honest folk.'

Babka smiled at him. 'If I were a witch your rope would not hold me. But I'm only a broom-maker, old enough to be your grandmother, so I'll walk with you. If we are going a long way you must lend me an arm, for I am old and my legs soon get tired.'

'We're going to the village where you'll be tried as a witch. Two men are waiting to give evidence against you. Come now and be silent. We'll tell you no more.'

Babka shook out her petticoats, smoothed her apron and hair.

'I'm ready,' she said.

'Look out!' warned the man in command. 'I know she looks as if butter wouldn't melt in her mouth, but I've been warned she's an artful one.'

'Who makes this charge against me?' asked Babka.

'The Queen. You'll know all in good time. Step out now.'

Babka said no more. She had displeased the Queen and, until she knew who was going to give evidence against her, there was nothing she could do but submit. Unless a miracle happened it was unlikely she would be saved, for the Queen was all-powerful and few would dare oppose her.

As they were about to enter the high road leading to the village Joseph came riding along, frantically whipping the old mare under him. Perspiration streamed down his face.

'Babka! Babka!' he shouted when he saw her. 'They say you are to be tried as a witch. They're building a great pile of wood outside the inn to burn you. What can I do to help? The village is full of soldiers and the Queen's special guards. Shall I fight these men and set you free?'

'No, Joseph! Ride as fast as you can to the palace and tell Janek, the magician's servant. But if nothing can be done do not interfere. You'll only get hurt, and you must think of Anna,' she commanded.

Joseph glared at the four men so fiercely that they began to draw their swords.

'I'll be back as soon as I can. If they hurt you, Babka, they'll have the village to reckon with,' he cried.

He wheeled round in a cloud of dust and was off down the road as fast as the old mare would take him.

'I told you this was going to be a nasty job,' said one of the men. 'I don't hold with burning an old woman, witch or no witch. Are you a witch, Babka?'

Babka laughed softly. 'Of course not. I have never harmed anyone in my life.'

'I don't believe you have,' replied the man, impressed by Babka's serene old face. 'Here, take my arm and I'll help you along. Now, don't we look a fine pair!' he said jokingly.

The man on the other side offered his arm also, and Babka accepted his help. She knew they would become more friendly if she let them help her, and she wanted all her strength for the ordeal to come.

'It is good of you to be kind to an old woman. I was growing tired. You walk faster than I do.'

'Let's sit by the roadside. It's pleasant in the sun and it's time to eat,' said the soldier in command.

He threw himself down on a grassy bank and the others did the same. They were no longer fearful or suspicious. One took a loaf of bread from his pouch, another a piece of sausage and the third a bottle of wine, and the food was

divided among them. Babka refused the wine but accepted a portion of bread and sausage.

'That is good sausage,' she said.

'My mother made it,' replied the soldier, pleased with her praise.

They ate together and this made them all friendly. They lingered over the meal, and Babka wondered if the men were deliberately dawdling to give Joseph time to fetch help.

When the last crumb had been eaten they went on their way to the village, and it never occurred to any of them that it was strange to be chatting in friendly fashion with an old woman who was to be tried as a witch at the end of their journey.

As they came in sight of the village, however, the leader said:

'We're the Queen's men. We must obey orders or lose our lives. And not only our lives, for the Queen would revenge herself upon our families if we disobeyed her. So we cannot help you. But if there's a chance – if your friends put up a fight – we'll do what we can; though a poor old woman like yourself stands little chance against the Queen.'

Babka thanked him, asked for a moment's pause to compose herself, then marched between her guards into the village street. The people streamed around her, an angry crowd, wild with excitement. Babka felt trouble brewing and her heart was full of dread. They had no weapons, only sticks and stones, whereas the Queen's men were armed. Moreover the Queen might wreak vengeance on them afterwards by burning their homes or making them pay a heavy fine.

A great pile of faggots and cord-wood stood on the green: there were stands for the judge and his officers, and others for the witnesses and the prisoner, the whole enclosed by a ring of guards. 'The Queen must think I'm important and dangerous to make all these preparations,' thought Babka.

The judge was waiting. She was to be tried, it seemed, according to the law of the land. The Queen did not mean the people to say it had not been a fair trial. Babka wondered again what possible evidence could be found to prove she was a witch. It was plain the village was on her side, so who could it be?

The trumpets sounded and the soldiers went round cuffing the villagers, the children and dogs into silence. Babka was pushed into her place by the four guards. She curtsied low to the judge, but when she stood up again she found her legs weak and trembling, and would have fallen had not one of the men given her a stool and signed to her to sit down.

'The woman is old and weak, your Excellency,' he said apologetically.

The judge frowned. The people began to mutter angrily. Babka looked so small and frail in that company of stalwart men. Then howls broke out afresh as the first witness appeared. It was Bat-Ears, shorn of his weapons and fine clothes, with his monstrous ears crimson in the sunlight.

'The woman is a witch, I swear it,' shouted Bat-Ears. 'She has a fire, a magic fire. It burned all night and was still bright in the morning, yet she put no wood on it. And she commanded the fire to come out and burn me, which it did. She captured me with magic. How could it be otherwise? I, Bat-Ears, to be beaten by a little old woman!'

Babka stood up to make her reply.

'He may be a big man, your Excellency, but he's a coward. He picked me up to put me on the fire and the wind blew down the chimney so that his clothes caught fire. I had to beat them out or he would have burnt to death. He rolled on the floor and cried like a baby until Joseph came and captured him,' said Babka in a strong clear voice all could hear.

The villagers shouted with joy at her words.

'Where is the man who captured the robber at the hut of the prisoner?' thundered the judge, looking with distaste at Bat-Ears, who was a deplorable sight with his head and shoulders covered with garbage the villagers had thrown at him.

There was some delay while the guards went to look for Joseph and the judge was getting impatient when Joseph appeared, his hair dark with perspiration and his clothes covered with the dust of hard riding. He apologized humbly for his dishevelled appearance, and this appeased the judge, who saw at once that Joseph was an honest man.

'Did you see this magic fire? Be quick now. You've already wasted the court's time,' he said sternly.

'There was a little fire in the hearth, your Excellency. The room was full of smoke from the burning clothes of the robber and he was lying on the floor crying with fright. He told me he had tried to put Babka on the fire. That was why his clothes got caught, and no wonder with all the frippery he was wearing. Instead of letting him burn, as she should have done, Babka beat out the flames with a broom.'

Joseph began to smile, a broad infectious smile.

'Forgive me, your Excellency, but it was very funny. Bat-Ears rolling on the floor squealing because Babka beat him so hard with a broom, he a big man and Babka a little old woman with no more strength than a kitten. We're very grateful to Babka. Bat-Ears has been frightening our womenfolk and robbing our homes.'

The villagers roared in agreement until the soldiers silenced them.

'Is this true?' thundered the judge, looking very terrible.

'Did you try to burn the prisoner? Did she put out the flames when your clothes caught fire? The truth, or it will be the worse for you.'

'Yes,' stuttered Bat-Ears, alarmed by the awful frown on the judge's face and frightened by the angry mutterings of the crowd.

'Take him back to prison. The man is a coward and a liar. His evidence is worth nothing. Bring on the next witness,' commanded the judge.

Babka lifted her eyes to see who the next witness would be. It was the red-haired dwarf, no longer ragged and dirty but dressed in the Queen's livery of silver and green. He had a feathered cap on his head and he took it off with a sweeping gesture as he bowed to the judge. Then he scowled as the muttering of the villagers broke out afresh.

'The ugly little toad! Babka took him in and fed him, and this is his gratitude,' one shouted over all the rest.

'You know this man?' the judge asked Babka.

'I do, your Excellency. I met him, ragged and starving, in the forest. I took him in and one day he ran away and I've never seen him since.'

'Did you give him cause to run away?' asked the judge.

'He has a violent temper. He wouldn't let the birds drink at the water-hole. As a punishment I gave the birds honey cakes I had brought him. He flew into a rage and tried to dam up the water, but when he found it would not stop flowing he ran away. I was glad he went. Whatever I did I could not make him happy.'

'You gave him honey cakes? You tried to make him happy?' asked the judge.

'He looked so miserable and he was always so bad-tempered, your Excellency.'

The judge turned to the dwarf. 'Is this true?' he asked.

'I ran away because she is a witch and I was afraid she

would harm me. Ah, she looks good and kind, but I know she's a witch. All the time I worked for her I never saw her tend the fire. It burned night and day and never went out. When she was in the village it burnt low and quiet, then when she came back it would flame and crackle to welcome her. She used to talk to it. "Burn fire and boil the soup," she would say, and the flames went leaping and set the pot boiling.'

The dwarf made a low bow to the judge and then leered triumphantly at Babka.

'You swear this?' asked the judge.

'I swear it, your Excellency.'

The judge looked at Babka. 'What have you to say? Does the dwarf speak the truth about the fire?'

'He does, your Excellency,' replied Babka quietly.

'How do you explain this fire which never goes out?'

'I can't,' replied Babka, and was silent.

'How do you explain this fire except by witchcraft?' asked the judge sternly.

Babka pondered a reply. How speak about the Golden Bird's gift when he had told her to be silent about it? And if she told her story would the judge believe her? She could only put her trust in the Golden Bird and hope that in some way he would come to her rescue as he had done before.

'I maintain that it is a fire produced by evil spells, and as you'll not tell us how it comes about, then you stand condemned as a witch,' shouted the judge.

'Oh no!' whispered Babka, looking round desperately for some sign of help.

The villagers, puzzled and afraid, were silent. Fear was in their eyes. Then from the back of the crowd came an old man, feeble and apparently half blind, led by Janek, the magician's servant.

'May I beg your Excellency to hear this witness?' asked

Janek, bowing humbly to the judge. 'He can explain this wonderful fire.'

Babka looked closely at the old man. He wore a rough smock and his head was covered by a high-crowned hat. In his hand he carried a bowl containing some smouldering pieces of wood, black as charcoal. It was the magician disguised. He gave her a warning look, then nodded his head foolishly, bowing and scraping before the judge.

'Let him speak,' commanded the judge.

'If your Excellency would let me speak for him? He is old and very slow,' pleaded Janek.

'Proceed,' snapped the judge, remembering the Queen's orders that Babka was to have a fair trial.

Janek bowed deeply, to the judge, to Babka, to the people who waited, silent and staring, to hear him.

'In this bowl are some pieces of wood. It is a special wood found only in one part of the forest, from one special tree. It is said that the tree was planted many hundreds of years ago by a wanderer from the far east. You see the piece that smoulders?'

Janek blew into the copper bowl so that the brand inside it flared with a sudden brilliance, and then shook it so that a few sparks fell to the ground.

'This piece of wood has been burning for many days. It will be many more days before it is burnt out. Babka, who has lived in the forest all her life, knows this tree and her fire was made of this special wood. That is why the dwarf did not see her make up the fire. If he had stayed longer he would have seen her replenish it. The old man and Babka are the only two people living who know where to find this tree, though some of you must have heard of it.'

Janek looked meaningly at Norbert, who could not bear the village to think there was anything about the forest he did not know.

'I've heard of it, your Excellency,' he shouted.

Others, not to be outdone and to help Babka, also shouted that they had heard old folk speak of this special tree.

'You also know,' went on Janek, speaking in a tense voice so that the crowd listened to him as if spellbound. 'You also know that this tree belongs to the Golden Bird and only dead and fallen branches may be gathered. So, naturally, there is very little of this special wood.'

'We know! We know!' cried the villagers in one voice.

'Why didn't you tell me about this wood?' the judge asked Babka.

'I was afraid of the Golden Bird, your Excellency,' replied Babka in a whisper.

The judge turned to the Queen's officer who was in charge of the trial. 'Have you any more witnesses who will swear the prisoner is a witch?' he asked impatiently.

'No. You have heard them all,' replied the officer.

'I cannot convict her on such flimsy evidence,' said the judge crossly. 'Babka, you are discharged. But beware! Next time you are suspected of evil practices you will not get off so lightly.'

Babka curtsied low. As she did so the villagers realized she was free and set up a howl of delight.

'We'd better get out of here before they remember there is a fire to be lighted and no one to burn on it,' whispered the Queen's officer to the judge. 'We must depart at once. The rabble might get ugly.'

He bid his men bring the horses and make ready to depart as quickly as possible.

The children had lit the pile of faggots and were dancing around it shouting with delight. In the excitement Babka and Joseph slipped away unnoticed through a farmyard into a quiet path leading to the forest. The magician and Janek had disappeared as soon as they had given their evidence. The rest of the villagers were enjoying themselves pelting the dwarf with rotten fruit and vegetables, and the guards surrounding the dwarf made no attempt to stop them. They perched him on a tall horse and grinned as they led him out of the village.

'I met Janek and the old man on the road. They were coming to your rescue, for they had heard of the trial at court,' said Joseph.

He would have liked to ask questions, about the fire, and about the magician, but Babka smiled at him affectionately and pointed to the sky where the sun was going down.

'We've been away all day, Joseph,' she said.

Joseph remembered his cows. 'The milking! With all this commotion nobody will think of them. I must leave you, Babka. You're quite safe now.'

'If the Queen had had her way I should have never seen the forest again, or my little house,' thought Babka, when she reached home.

She fed her birds and stood for a few moments looking into the dark forest, breathing the cool, pine-scented air gratefully. It was good to be home again, but she could not help wondering where the Queen would strike next.

Chapter Eight

Babka goes to the Palace

The harvest was poor that year and a hard winter followed for the people of the forest. If their good King had been on the throne he would have given them corn from the palace granaries as he had done in other bad years, but the Queen refused to help them. There was nothing to do but wait for the spring to bring the rain and make the crops grow.

But when at last the spring came it did not bring rain but a cold dry wind, parching the earth and turning it into yellow dust in which nothing would grow. The streams ran dry, and the wide river beyond the village turned to a shallow, evil-smelling marsh, its clear waters changed to yellow mud. There was famine in the villages of the forest and the cattle drooped and died in the desolate fields. Behind closed doors and in secret places people whispered that the drought and famine were caused by the Queen. It was said that she had tried to rule the wind and the rain and this was Nature's revenge.

The clearing round Babka's hut was the only green patch for many miles. Here the water-drops from the little fountain in the water-hole sprinkled the grass, so that it made a thick green carpet where the birds still played.

Babka filled her bucket at the fountain and watered her beans and potatoes. Her heart was heavy when she thought of her friends in the village growing lean and grey with

hunger, their beasts dying and their crops ruined. Her little patch could feed so few of them.

The idea came to Babka to go and see the Prince. He might be able to help the people if he knew of their plight. But first she had to plan how she could speak to the Prince unknown to the Queen and the rest of the court. She knew that if the Queen discovered she was in the palace she would be lost. It meant putting herself within the enemy's gates, but Babka decided to risk it. To do nothing while her friends starved was impossible. Only in the forest was she safe, where she was protected by the Golden Bird. She would have to be very careful indeed.

Babka packed a basket with fresh cucumbers and salad from her garden. Under these things she placed a spray of leaves from the chestnut sapling growing by her door. She had watered the little tree every day, and unlike the rest of the forest, its leaves were green and fresh.

Her basket packed, she set off on her long journey. Her plan was to keep to the forest paths and, if possible, reach the outskirts of the palace grounds without being seen. The Queen had many spies and Babka knew that since the trial her movements had been watched.

All day she journeyed, stopping only for short periods to eat and rest. It was evening when she entered on the last mile of her long walk. So far it had been simple; now she must keep her wits about her. Janek, the magician's servant, would help her. He was a resourceful lad and could be trusted.

She left the forest for the high road following the great stone wall of the palace grounds. At intervals along the wall were strong gates guarded by sentries. Putting her shawl over her head Babka approached the gates. A soldier with a drawn sword barred her way.

'What do you want so late in the day, old woman?' he asked.

'I want to speak with Janek, the servant of the magician,' replied Babka in a timid quavering voice.

'What do you want with him?'

'I'm his aunt,' said Babka.

'If you're begging for food you'd best be off,' grumbled the sentry.

Babka took her basket from under her shawl. 'I haven't come to beg. I've brought him a present,' she said, letting the cloth slip so that he could see the contents of her basket.

The sentry's eyes went wide with astonishment when he saw the fresh green cucumbers and the little white and red radishes.

'Where did you get them? It's precious little fresh food we sentries get. Salt pork and dried beans.... I haven't tasted a cucumber this year....'

'I'm a poor old woman and this is all I have left. I want to see Janek once more before I die. He always tells me my cucumbers are the best in the land. If you'll bring him to me I'll give you a cucumber and a bunch of radishes,' Babka said, watching the sentry's face.

'I'm not allowed to leave my post. But give me a cucumber and I'll let you in. You see the tower over there? That's where the magician lives.'

Babka pulled her shawl over her face and hurried to the tower. The path was edged with dark trees that held the gathering dusk, but she could see a torch blazing over the entrance to the tower and she could only hope that none of the guards would recognize her.

Two of them were playing at dice on a broad stone in the doorway. They stood up quickly and clanked their swords when they saw Babka coming.

'What do you want, old woman? Strangers are not allowed in the palace grounds after dark.'

'I've come to see Janek, my nephew. I've a little present for him, and for you if you'll let me in.'

'Can't be done! Queen's orders.'

'Then go and tell Janek his aunt wishes to see him,' she begged. 'I'm an old woman. I wish to see Janek before I die. Grant an old woman this last wish,' she entreated, and held out two cucumbers.

The soldiers looked at them longingly, then one took them and pushed her quickly inside the door where it was dark and shadowy.

'Wait there. Janek will be coming with his master's supper presently. Don't make a sound and keep out of sight.'

Babka crouched in the darkness. She was so still that after a few moments the soldiers forgot her and began to play at dice again, gambling for the cucumbers.

After a little while she crept towards the stone steps going up inside the tower. She knew the magician's room was at the very top. Tucking up her skirts she ran lightly up the first flight and the noise she made might have been a scurrying mouse or a dead leaf in the breeze. She paused to listen. The sentries were still busy with their game and had not heard her. She ran swiftly up the next flight and paused again, but all was quiet. She did the same after climbing the third flight and then, shaking out her skirts, she walked quietly up the remaining steps, shuddering a little at the slimy dankness of the walls.

She was exhausted by the time she reached the top, but she pushed open the door of the magician's room and slipped inside. The magician was there, muttering to himself over the fire as he tried a new spell to bring rain. The creaking of the door roused him and he looked up, his eyes full of fear.

'The Queen does not know you are here?' he asked anxiously.

Babka shook her head. 'I want to speak to the Prince. As soon as I've spoken to him I'll go away again,' replied Babka.

'You must rest and eat and drink after your journey. Janek will tell the Prince you are here,' said the magician, still looking troubled. 'The Queen must not find you . . .'

Janek came in at that moment and he beamed with pleasure when he saw Babka.

'My aunt with the cucumbers? I knew it must be you, Babka. I told the sentries you were a vision conjured up by my master. Now they will not come looking for you. I told them the cucumbers were magic also.' He held them out triumphantly saying, 'It doesn't do to let the court know our business.'

'You did well, my boy. Be quick and put the supper on the table. Babka wants to see the Prince. You must find him at once and give him the message,' said the magician.

'I'll need a bribe. And our purse is empty,' replied Janek.

Babka handed him the gold piece she had brought with her, the last one from the robber's bag. Then she took the spray of chestnut leaves from the basket.

'Give this to the Prince and he will know who sent them,' she said.

Janek smiled. 'Leave it to me. I'll return as soon as I can. Be patient. It is not easy to speak with the Prince without the Queen's spies being aware of it. We say in the palace she has a thousand eyes and a thousand ears. But tonight she is giving a ball and is busy entertaining her guests – with food that would keep a hundred poor people from starving,' he added bitterly.

It was midnight when Janek returned. He was carrying a black cloak over his arm.

'The Prince will see you in the forest outside the palace,' he said as he wrapped the cloak around Babka. 'I will take you to him on my horse. We shall have no trouble with the sentries, for I've given them something in their wine to make them sleep.'

'If you want to help the people, find the Grey Gander,' murmured the magician as Babka bade him farewell.

He would say no more so they left him turning the crystal round and round in his thin bony hands and moaning to himself.

'My master is very strange these days,' said Janek. 'Something troubles him.'

Babka was too anxious about her mission to worry about the magician. Not until they had passed the sleeping sentries at the gate and were well away from the palace did she wonder for a moment why the magician had told her to find the Grey Gander.

The Prince was waiting for them in the forest. He listened sadly when she told him about the starving villagers.

'If my father were here it would be different. But I have no power to oppose the Queen and open the granaries. But there is something I can do. Now listen carefully.

'I am going to send you a little white cow and a sack of meal that were given to me by a wise woman when I journeyed east some years ago. The cow will continue to give milk as long as each person takes only one small pailful at each milking. If anyone takes more than that the cow will disappear. As to the sack of meal, each person can fill a small bowl once a day between dawn and sunset. It will renew itself each night, but if any is spilt or wasted then it will shrink and remain empty for ever. You are the only person I can trust with the cow and the sack. Now I must go. The Queen must not discover that I have left the palace. All would be lost if she knew.'

The Prince mounted his horse and rode quickly away.

'You've a long and weary journey before you, Babka.

Will you take my horse?' asked Janek when the Prince had gone.

'I can go more quietly through the forest on foot. The Prince has renewed my strength. But before you go can you tell me why the magician said I was to find the Grey Gander?'

Janek shook his head. 'My master has many secrets. Lately even his fear of the Queen has changed. He sees things in the crystal that frighten him. I fear his wits are gone. If he were not so old and helpless I should leave him and ask the Prince to take me into his service, but without me the old man would starve.'

'You're a good lad, Janek. Your reward will come one day,' replied Babka. Then she thanked him again and set off on her long walk home.

Chapter Nine

The Little White Cow

The dawn was breaking over the forest when Babka arrived home. She was footsore and exhausted by her long journey, but she felt happier now that she knew she would be able to help her friends in the village.

As she was making herself a meal she heard a plaintive mooing outside the hut and there, on the grassy plot by the water-hole, was a small white cow, a gentle beast who came towards her asking to be milked. Babka stroked her gently. 'You're very welcome, my pretty one,' she whispered.

News of the wonderful white cow and the never-failing sack of meal soon went round the village. Every morning at daybreak the villagers appeared for their milk and meal, and some took turns to watch and see that no one took more than their share. A few looked at Babka suspiciously, murmuring she was a witch and that witch's food would do them no good, but their hunger was too strong, and soon they were taking their pail of milk and bowl of meal like the rest.

For a few days all went well. The children began to look plump and rosy again and played around the water-hole so that the clearing rang with their games and laughter. The mothers gossiped together praising the rich milk and the goodness of the meal. Babka was very happy. Famine had been averted and her friends saved.

But the fame of Babka's cow spread and soon strangers began to come from villages far away. Babka found it difficult to control them. Some were rough and rude, and when the people of her own village tried to make them take their turn with the others they fought with sticks and knives.

As these strangers came a long way they could not return to their homes at night, so they camped near the hut. Night and day Babka had to keep watch. Only the fear that Babka was a witch kept them from stealing the cow and the sack.

She had no rest, for they began to milk the cow as soon as there was light in the sky and continued until darkness fell. It was always noisy in the forest now and Babka had no time for her birds or her garden. The strangers stole her vegetables, trampling her neat garden into a dusty wilderness. They cut down the forest trees to make their fires, and the birds, frightened by the noise and the traps set to snare them, abandoned the place.

One day when Babka was watching them take meal from the sack she heard a great uproar around the little cow. It came from a band of rough men who had descended on the clearing armed with clubs and knives and who had frightened away most of the villagers. Babka had begged them to stay and guard the cow, but the mothers had gathered their children together and fled, and their menfolk had followed them to see them safely through the forest, so that only Babka and the band of ruffians had been left.

With this band of rough men there was an old woman, her hair falling about her face in wild elf-locks and who had a loud jeering voice which stirred her companions into a frenzy of destruction. It was this old woman who was milking the cow, that stood with twitching tail and a look of alarm in her mild brown eyes.

'You are taking more than your share. You're spilling the milk,' Babka heard someone shout.

She hurried to the cow, but it was too late. For the first time she saw the woman clearly, and one glance told her everything. It was the Queen, disguised in a coarse grey wig, ragged clothes and a stained face. She was milking the cow not into a pail but into a sieve so that as fast as the milk poured into the sieve it ran out again and was wasted.

Babka went to lead the cow away but the animal gave an angry toss of the head, mooed loudly and with a kick which sent the Queen flying she was away into the forest. In a moment she had disappeared.

The Queen picked herself up and laughed in Babka's face.

'There goes your cow,' she screamed. 'Call her back if you can!'

Then with a swift movement the Queen reached the sack and emptied it on the ground spilling the meal in the dust.

'And there goes your sack of meal. Fill it again if you can,' she shouted triumphantly.

Babka picked up the empty sack and shook it helplessly. The Queen had defeated her.

'Fools!' laughed the Queen. 'Fools! To be taken in by a witch! Make her call back the cow and refill the sack!' And she laughed again while Babka stood helpless and despairing.

More people had arrived by this time, some of them from her own village.

'We want the cow,' they shouted, filled with anger and disappointment.

'We're hungry and you said you would feed us,' they cried.

There was not one friendly face in the crowd. Even her own villagers had turned against her. The Queen took advantage of this. She began to rouse the people with her

cry of 'Burn the witch! Burn the witch! Burn her on her own fire!'

Soon they were echoing the cry, maddened by excitement, while the ruffians who had come with the Queen began to press Babka back into her hut. The clearing was full of shouting angry people who fought and pushed like wild creatures. And all the time the Queen urged them on.

Babka was helpless. She was being forced towards the open hearth where her fire burned steadily. She looked around for help but she could see only the evil face of the Queen and her wicked band, while the few villagers watched helpless in the background.

'Golden Bird, take back your gift before it destroys me,' Babka whispered in despair, as she was pushed nearer the flames.

In an instant the fire went black and dead. The ashes which had been glowing before were grey. Babka felt them cold about her feet and ankles. One of the men being pushed from behind fell forward and as he touched the dead fire he let out a wild yell of fear. He called to the others to let the witch go before she turned them all into stone. 'The fire was dead,' he screamed. 'The witch would never burn.'

Panic seized the crowd as it turned to run away. The Queen was the first to go, fighting her way out like a mad creature. The others followed, until in a few moments the clearing was empty except for a few stragglers who had been hurt in the scrum. They went limping off, too frightened to feel their injuries and anxious only to get away.

Babka watched the last of them disappear, her heart heavy with bitterness. A great silence, the first for many days, fell upon the forest. The Queen had done her work well. The little white cow had gone, the sack of meal lay empty for ever.

Babka went into the hut. Utterly weary and without hope she lay down on her bed in the corner and fell into a deep exhausted sleep.

Chapter Ten

Babka seeks the Grey Gander

Babka awoke the next morning to the sound of a fire crackling. For a moment she thought she must be dreaming, for had not the Golden Bird put out her fire? She opened her eyes and saw Janek busy on the hearth.

'Wake up, Babka,' he called, seeing her move. 'I've good news for you.'

'I thought my fire was out,' Babka said.

'There was one smouldering stick. I fetched more wood and now it burns well,' replied Janek.

Babka was comforted. The Golden Bird had not entirely deserted her but had left one stick to show he was still her friend.

'The story of how they tried to burn you as a witch reached the palace, and as the Queen returned home sick the magician sent me to find out what had happened,' said Janek. 'And what do I find? Babka sleeping as peacefully as a child while the Queen is tossing on her bed scorched and shrivelled and the courtiers wagging their tails with delight because she is helpless. Ah! You're clever, Babka! It takes more than the Queen, with all her spells, to burn you.'

Janek respectfully handed her a bowl of porridge he had made.

'The little white cow is gone and the meal sack is empty,' replied Babka sadly. 'Now the people will starve.'

'Greedy fools! It's useless to try to help them,' snapped Janek. 'Look what they did to you when you tried!'

'I failed,' said Babka. 'You must tell the Prince.'

'He knows. He's taken wagons and horses and men to fetch corn from the granaries beyond the river. Now, eat your porridge. I've a message for you from my master.'

Babka did as she was told, smiling at Janek. It was pleasant to be waited upon.

'If the Queen is sick and the Prince away . . .' she began.

'Exactly. My master says the Queen will not recover. It is the vengeance of the Golden Bird – because she tried to interfere with his gift to you. There are those in the palace who might try to steal the throne before the Prince returns. My master is old and feeble and he has a great sin on his conscience. He says you alone can help him.'

'But what can I do? If only the King were to come back . . .'

'That's it. The King. His disappearance was some mischief wrought by the Queen.'

'Does the magician know what happened to the King?' asked Babka.

'He knows, but as long as the Queen lives he dare not tell. He sits turning the crystal round and round and all he will say is, "Tell Babka to find the Grey Gander."'

'Where am I to look? And how can the Grey Gander help us?' asked Babka.

Janek shook his head. 'There is deep meaning in these words. It is for you to read the riddle. I know nothing more. I wish I did.'

Babka arose and shook out her skirts. She looked at the hearth. The sticks Janek had put on had burnt away, but one glowing red piece remained.

'Tell your master I will go and seek the Grey Gander,' she replied.

'It's our only hope,' replied Janek gravely. 'Now I must go. If the Queen dies anything might happen.'

Babka watched him ride away and was sad to see him go. Now she was quite alone. The magician had said find the Grey Gander, but where was she to look? Those birds who had not died in the famine had flown far away. Where could she begin the search? Babka looked at the chestnut sapling which had miraculously survived the trampling crowds. She stroked the slim stem gently.

As she did so a breeze rustled the tuft of leaves. She saw a light film of cloud had formed over the harsh blue sky empty for so many rainless days. 'The wind is changing,' she told herself. 'Soon the rain will come and refresh the earth.'

Cheered by the thought she began to make ready for her journey. She took the small glowing brand from the hearth and placed it in an iron pot. Then she slung the sack over her shoulder and taking up the little pot set out on her travels.

'I'll follow the first bird I see,' she told herself.

As she spoke an old crow with a ragged tail flew out of a tree in front of her. He gave a hoarse croak, flew ahead for a few yards, then cocked a bright inquiring eye at her.

Babka delved into her pocket, found a crumb of cheese and threw it to him. He pounced on it eagerly, then flew on again, and settled once more for her to catch up with him. Babka threw him another crumb, amused at his antics, and he repeated the performance, flying ahead and waiting for her to catch up.

And so she went on, the crow flying a long distance each time until by the time the cheese was all eaten she had gone many miles from her hut and was in a part of the forest unknown to her.

'I suppose you'll leave me now the cheese is finished?' Babka said.

The old crow croaked, turning his head as if to tell her to

follow him. Babka did so and was surprised to find how cool and green the path was, with the leaves of the trees still fresh and bright, unlike her own parched brown part of the forest.

'It would be pleasant to sit and rest,' thought Babka, who had walked many miles by now and was feeling tired. But the old crow would not let her rest. He kept up loud complaining croaks, flew off and then came back, obviously urging her to follow him.

So she plodded on, the bird leading the way. Then, suddenly, when she felt she could walk no longer, she saw, under a great spreading oak, a little round hut with walls of turf and a roof of straw and a fire of sticks just outside the hole which served the hut for a door.

The crow flapped onto the roof with a joyous croak and folded his wings, and a little old woman appeared at the door of the hut waving a wooden spoon.

'So you're come back at last, you black imp,' she shouted.

The crow put his head under his wing as if he were sleeping. He looked so comical that Babka, tired as she was, could not help laughing.

'Come and sit down, Babka,' said the little old woman, showing no surprise at Babka's presence.

Babka sat down on a log of wood and the old woman ladled out a bowl of soup from the pot on the fire.

'Eat your soup. It will revive you,' she said.

'It is good soup,' said Babka, sipping it gratefully.

When the meal was over Babka asked Nonno, for that was the old woman's name, if she knew where to find the Grey Gander. Nonno shook her head.

'My sister Bonno, who lives in the far north, would know. All the wild birds who come from the frozen lands call on her in the autumn as they journey south. The wild swans and the geese, they tell her all their news.'

'Where can I find her?' asked Babka.

'Krak shall go with you and show you the way. He's my messenger,' replied Nonno, pointing to the old crow. 'To-night you stay here and in the morning we'll prepare you for the journey, for it is long and hard and very cold.'

Babka shivered, afraid of leaving the forest for the desolate north. Yet she must find the Grey Gander and this was the only lead she had.

Babka stayed with Nonno for two days and nights, for Nonno refused to let her depart until she was thoroughly rested and preparations for the journey were complete. When at last everything was ready Babka gasped to see the load Nonno expected her to carry. There was a sack of food, a padded quilt and felt boots to keep her warm, the glowing brand in the iron pot and a large jar of honey as a gift for Bonno.

Nonno laughed when she saw Babka's look of dismay. She put two fingers in her mouth and gave a shrill whistle. Three times she whistled and in a few moments a sturdy, creamy-white pony appeared. Babka patted his arched neck and stroked his long nose. 'So you are to carry me,' she murmured.

'Grue loves a journey,' explained Nonno, arranging the packages in the saddle-bags and tying the iron pot carefully where it would not touch the pony's flank.

Babka mounted, thanked Nonno for her kindness and with Krak flying ahead as guide she set off.

As long as they kept to the narrow paths of the forest Grue stepped carefully, but once on the open plain he began to gallop. With hoofs barely touching the ground he sped along, tail and mane streaming behind him, only pulling up when Babka asked him to stop.

Seven days they journeyed, stopping at dusk at any spot which gave them a little shelter from the cold wind that blew across the empty waste, and then on again at dawn. Each day the wind grew colder and the night frosts more severe. Babka was very glad of the little fire in the iron pot. It warmed her soup and made each place they rested in at night seem more homelike.

At last they came to the cave where Bonno lived. Around the cave the ground was strewn with large grey rocks and tangles of shrubby thorny bushes. Some of the rocks had strange shapes like crouching monsters turned to stone.

Grue picked his way delicately now, and Krak flew ahead croaking loudly. Stirring a pot over a fire at the entrance to the cave was a little old woman, very much like Nonno except that she wore so many clothes to keep her warm that she was wider than she was tall. She shouted a welcome as they approached and Krak settled on her shoulder and folded his wings. She spoke to him caressingly and he replied softly in a purr of pleasure. Babka knew she was meeting a friend who also loved birds.

Bonno helped her to dismount, for Babka was stiff with the long ride. She felt at home at once. Bonno handed her a bowl of hot soup from the pot on the fire, and told her to sit down on a sheepskin by the fire. 'Drink this, while I feed Grue. Then we can talk,' Bonno said.

When Bonno returned, Babka asked her if she had seen the Grey Gander.

'We will ask the wild geese. I'm expecting them at any time now,' Bonno said. 'Come with me and we'll watch for their coming.'

She picked up the sheepskin and wrapped it round Babka. And as she went with Bonno Babka saw that beyond the cave the ground sloped down to a large shallow lake gleaming like silver in the dusk. The lake had a sandy shore, but above the water-line the ground was covered with thin wiry grass and clumps of rough bushes. They could hear the

restless movements of hundreds of small birds in the bushes as they passed.

'The birds are beginning to come from the north,' said Bonno. 'They rest here awhile before they go south. But listen!'

Babka listened and heard in the far distance the faint honking of wild geese and, as they came nearer, the sound of hundreds of beating wings.

Bonno gripped Babka's arm. 'Hush! Do not speak or move. They are afraid of strangers,' she whispered.

The sound of the wings became louder, a steady rhythm as they beat the air. In the pale sky Babka could see the dark shapes of wild geese flying in formation above the water. The formation broke up when it reached the centre of the lake, and the birds began to descend, calling to each other as they glided down. For a few moments there was tumult, the sound of wings and voices mingling, those on the water calling to those in the sky and one bird answering another. Then the sky was empty and on the lake the bobbing figures rose and fell on the gentle waves, their voices softer now that all were safely landed.

'Stay here,' commanded Bonno. 'I'll talk to them. They are the shyest birds in the world. If they are frightened they'll rise again and we shall find out nothing.'

Babka stood waiting while Bonno went down to the water's edge. When she came back she shook her head sadly.

'The geese tell me that two of their company haven't arrived, a grey gander and a goose. The gander is a stranger who has never made the winter journey before; his strength failed and he dropped to the ground. His goose remained with him. They had to leave them, for to stay in the north with winter coming meant death and starvation for all.'

'You think he's the Grey Gander?' asked Babka.

'I only know he is a stray bird who joined their company in the marshes last year. But although he's a stranger they speak of him with respect.'

'I must go and look for him,' said Babka.

They were turning back to the cave when the wild geese on the lake began to call loudly, and some rose from the water flapping their wings. Soon the lake was in an uproar with their cries.

'Look!' commanded Bonno. 'Look!'

Babka looked into the sky and heard the faint wild cry of a bird, a solitary melancholy note. The geese on the water answered. They watched a bird coming down, heard the excited welcome of the others and then there was silence again.

'Is that the Grey Gander?' asked Babka.

'No! It's the young goose. She has left him behind,' replied Bonno. 'But I will talk to them again.'

Bonno went to the water's edge and when she returned she took Babka by the arm and led her to the cave.

'It's a long story, and you're cold,' she said kindly.

Chapter Eleven

Babka finds the King

Bonno stirred the fire and set the firelight dancing about the cave.

'Come and warm yourself,' she said to Babka, whose face was blue with cold.

'Tell me about the Grey Gander,' begged Babka. 'We're wasting time. I must set out to find him at once. Unless he's already dead? Was that why the young goose left him?'

'He's not dead. Be patient. You cannot go into the frozen north without preparation. You would lose yourself and freeze to death. But before I tell you about the Grey Gander I have good news for you. Rain has come to the forest country. The wild geese told me.'

'They have come from the far north. How can they know?'

Bonno laughed. 'They know everything about the weather. Snow in the far north means rain in the forest. They also told me the Queen is dead.'

'The Queen dead!' repeated Babka. 'Did the wind tell them that also?'

'It was the young goose, the one who stayed with the Grey Gander, who told me. The Queen is dead and the King is found!'

Babka stared at Bonno in amazement and joy. Now all would be well in the forest country.

'It was like this,' Bonno continued. 'When the goose

stayed behind with the Grey Gander she urged him again and again to fly with her, but he was too exhausted. So she sat beside him in the shelter of a great rock which stands alone on the plain many miles from this place. She knew his strength was failing but she would not leave him to die alone.'

'She was risking her own life to stay with him?'

'Of course,' replied Bonno sharply. 'Geese are faithful to their mates. But to get on with my story. It happened like this. The Grey Gander stood up and stretched his wings to try once more to fly with her when, as she watched, in his place stood a man. A wild goose is afraid of man, so, finding herself alone, she was frightened and flew on. She wanted the comfort of her companions.'

'So the Grey Gander was the King. Already he may be freezing to death on the plain. He has no horse or fire, nothing but the shelter of the rock to protect him from the cold. How shall I find him? You must help me. The goose must show me the way,' cried Babka desperately.

Bonno shook her head.

'The goose will not return to the north until next spring. A king means nothing to her. She flew due south to reach the lake, so you must travel due north to reach the King.'

'But there are no landmarks to help me. Only the plain on all sides. How shall I know I'm going in the right direction? In the forest I can find my way – but here! What shall I do?'

'There is the northern star,' replied Bonno. 'Keep that before you all the way and you cannot get lost.'

She went to the door of the cave and drew aside the curtains of skins. 'See, in the sky the bright star that never moves, the constant one. It will be your guide.'

Then she fetched Grue and filled the panniers with food and warm clothing and hung the iron pot on the saddle. She

gave Babka a cap and cloak of feathers to keep her warm. She promised to send a message to Janek by Krak, the crow, to tell him to let the Prince know about the King and where to find him.

At first Grue did not want to leave the warm cave, but Babka encouraged him with soft words and after a few moments he tossed his mane and began to gallop.

'On, Grue, on!' urged Babka. 'As fast as you can, little one, to save the King!'

The pony flew on, his neat little hoofs striking sparks from the frozen ground, his breath smoking from his nostrils. Keeping the star as their guide they rode on through the night, hour after hour, until Grue began to flag and Babka was chilled and stiff beneath her cloak of feathers. The stars had begun to wane and a pale silvery light gave way to a sullen grey daylight.

They rested a few hours and with the star's reappearance in the sky were off again, and now Babka began to search the horizon for the great rock where the wild goose had left the King. They saw it looming up in the twilight and reached it in one last wild gallop.

An overhanging shelf a few feet from the ground made a kind of roof and a mound of earth had been piled up to make a wind-break. They saw the King, cold and stiff, lying on a bed of twigs gathered from the shrubby bushes on the plain.

Babka knelt by his side. Was she too late? His hands were deathly cold and his face was blue. She piled some of the twigs on the smouldering brand in the iron pot. She covered him with the padded quilt and the feathered cloak. Soon the twigs caught alight and the air in the little recess became warmer.

Grue liked the warmth also. He squeezed himself into a corner and munched the cake Babka gave him, and the warmth of his body also helped to defeat the freezing cold of their shelter. Babka bustled about, preparing soup, gathering what fuel she could from the dry bushes, tugging at the roots to find enough to feed her little fire.

'Golden Bird, be kind,' she entreated, as she tended the fire, and the smouldering brand began to glow with a fierce heat that warmed them all.

But the King remained motionless and his hands and feet were still cold. Babka heated small stones in the fire and put them at his feet. Then, when she had done all she could, she sat down by the fire and waited. Grue slept with drooping head and tail, and outside their warm shelter the frozen silence was like the silence of death.

Babka, lulled by the warmth, fell into an uneasy doze, and then into a deep sleep. As she slept the snow began to fall in a continuous piling of soft flake on soft flake making two more walls, so that when she awoke their shelter now had four walls and was lit by the glistening whiteness of newly fallen snow.

Babka put out her hand and felt the King. He was warm and the pinched look had vanished from his face. He was breathing now in a peaceful sleep.

She put the pot on the fire again and soon the little shelter was filled with the smell of good onion soup strengthened by chips of dried fish Bonno had given her. The King stirred and opened his eyes. His fingers touched the soft feathers of her cloak stretched over him.

'What is this?' he asked in a weak voice. 'I lay down to die and I awake to find myself in a snow hut with a cooking-pot on the fire and an old woman tending it. Are you a dream?'

'I'm Babka, the broom-maker, your Majesty,' she replied. Lack of space made it impossible to curtsey but she bent her head in humble salute.

She filled her wooden bowl with soup and gave it to him. 'It will give you strength,' she said.

The King smiled and tried to sit up and drink, but he was so weak that he fell back again. As if he were an ailing child Babka fed him slowly and carefully.

'More, more,' he whispered. 'I'm starving.'

'You must wait a little. It's not good to take too much at first,' warned Babka.

'You're a wise old woman,' replied the King, and his voice sounded stronger. 'How warm it is! I thought I should never feel warm again!'

Grue startled them by neighing loudly.

'Are you warning us of something?' asked Babka.

The pony went to the snow wall which had formed while they had been sleeping. He broke it down with his forefeet. Babka looked outside. She could see nothing but whirling snow which froze on her eyelids when she poked her head through the hole Grue had made.

'A blizzard! He knew it was coming, and so did the wild geese.'

Babka tucked up her skirts and went outside. Quickly she began to work forming the snow into blocks and building a strong wall against the increasing wind. She strengthened the three sides of the shelter, and when she had done all she could she crawled back through the small hole she had left for a door and closed it also. Let the blizzard blow with all its might, they would be safe in their little snow house, three sides made of snow blocks and one wall and a roof of stone. They could not be blown away.

'When the blizzard is over we shall have to dig ourselves out,' she said.

'You take it very calmly,' replied the King.

Babka smiled as she poured out another bowl of soup for him.

'Drink this. It will help to make you strong,' she said.

The King drank and lay down again and slept. Babka fed Grue, who stood shivering and miserable. He hated being shut up in the little snow house. Babka talked to him soothingly.

'Be patient, Grue. Soon you'll be back with Nonno. You shall have corn and sweet hay and the King will give you a harness hung with silver bells,' she said.

And in a little while Grue was comforted and he slept also, while outside the cruel wind howled about their tiny shelter and the snow piled up around it.

Chapter Twelve

The King tells his Story

The King was restless. 'How long before we can leave here, Babka? I keep thinking of the palace and my people,' he said.

Outside the blizzard still raged. Babka knew that if it lasted much longer they would die of starvation, for their food was nearly all gone.

'We can only wait and hope,' she replied.

'If there was something we could do to make the waiting less tedious?' complained the King.

'If your Majesty would tell me your story,' Babka suggested timidly. 'It would help us to forget how hungry we are.'

The King smiled at her. 'It will also help me to remember that, but for you, I should now be lying frozen to death under the snow,' he replied. 'Come closer and I'll begin.

'It was my own fault. I have brought all my troubles on myself. I knew the Queen hated me. I knew she wanted to get rid of me because I was the only one who stood in the way of her practising her magic openly. And she dare not oppress the people while I was King. Yet I let her deceive me.'

The King sighed and stared miserably into the fire.

'That's why I'm cooped up here, like an animal in a hole, while my people are without a ruler. Because I offended the Golden Bird to please my wicked Queen.'

'The Golden Bird!' whispered Babka, looking at the glowing fire, which seemed to leap into sudden light as the King spoke.

'The Golden Bird has always been the protector of our family and of our good name. We wear his crest upon the crown, we bear it on our standards in battle. The Queen hated and feared him because his power was greater than hers. She was always plaguing me about him, telling me that if I loved her I would bring her one small feather from his golden plumage. More than anything else she coveted a feather from the Golden Bird.'

'Why?' asked Babka.

'Because it would give her a little power over him. I know that now. But when she said that if I would give her one feather she would become a good Queen and forsake her magic I believed her. I asked her how I could take one of his feathers? I could not ask him, for I never saw him except from afar.

'"You can shoot. You're always boasting what a good archer you are. Can't you shoot one feather from his tail without hurting him?" she kept saying, taunting and tormenting me. In the end I began to believe that if I got her one feather she would be satisfied and become a good Queen.

'I began to practise shooting at the ravens in the park until at last I could shoot one feather from their tails without hurting them. And the Queen kept telling me what a good archer I was until I became very proud of myself. Do you think I was very foolish, Babka?' asked the King.

But Babka refused to answer, and the King went on with his story. 'I should have known she was false, but I was foolish and vain. I loved her and her praise made me proud so that all I could think of was shooting that one feather from the tail of the Golden Bird.

'The next thing was to find him. There was one place where he sometimes appeared, and that was on a tall fir tree in the palace gardens. The evening sun used to catch the top of the tree before it went down behind the forest, and the Golden Bird would perch there and let the sun light up his crimson and gold plumage so that he seemed to glow as if on fire.

'This tree was not too far from the top of the old tower, and so I made my plans. For several evenings I watched from the tower, telling nobody but the Queen why I did so. The old magician lives up there and I commanded him to stop in his room until I had gone. He tried to warn me. He guessed what I was going to do, or the Queen had told him. But I refused to listen. I was waiting for the right evening, when the sky was clear and there would be a golden sunset.

'At last it came. I went up the tower while the Queen waited below. Everyone else was banished from the palace grounds. The magician came to the door of his room as I passed, whispering to me not to shoot, but I gave him a great push and sent him staggering away. Then I went out onto the balcony afraid I might be too late. It had to be just the right moment, with the Golden Bird in just the right position.'

The King stopped, re-living the evening in his mind, while Babka waited silently.

'Then I saw him flying with outstretched wings towards the tower, floating in the golden air enjoying the power of his wings and the serene sky. It was so clear that I could almost pick out each beautiful feather. I took careful aim, and as if he knew what I meant to do he spread out his golden tail like a great fan. One golden feather drifted down, spinning like a leaf to the ground. I watched it, full of pride, and then looked for the Golden Bird, but he had gone.

'Then I knew I had done a terrible thing. I wanted to fly after the bird and ask his forgiveness. But there was nothing I could do. My exultant mood changed to sorrow. Behind me the magician was wringing his hands and wailing, while the Queen below twirled the golden feather in her fingers, chanting some strange song.

'Suddenly I hated her. She had planned this thing for my undoing. By giving her a feather from the Golden Bird I had put myself in her power and had lost his protection perhaps for ever. I would kill her and that crazy old magician and rid the country of their evil spells.

'But when I came to move I found I was helpless. My sword fell on the stones and I could not pick it up. My arms had changed to wings and my feet were webbed. The only sound I could make was a strangled hiss. My body was covered with grey feathers. I had been changed into the Grey Gander. The terrible thing was that I still knew I was the King yet I was powerless to ask anyone for help. The only one who could help me was the Golden Bird, and I had offended him beyond hope of pardon.

'Very soon I had to fly for my life. The Queen had sent her men to look for a grey gander and bring him to her dead or alive. I managed to escape and hid in the forest, only flying after dark. I made all kinds of plans. I hoped I could see the Queen walking alone in the palace garden as she often did, and then I would beat her to death with my strong wings. But she was cunning and never went unattended. She kept the windows of her apartment closed, and always there were men seeking to find and kill me.

'So in the end I gave up trying and joined a flock of geese in the marshes. It was safer; among a flock of geese one grey gander was like any other. There seemed no other life for me but that of a wild bird. I could only grieve for my people, I could not help them. The rest you know, Babka.

How I flew north with the flock, and then on our way south again I became exhausted and the young goose stayed with me. Until, when the Queen died, the spell was broken and I became a man again, alone in this vast frozen waste.'

The King looked at Babka sitting quietly beside him.

'And then you came and saved my life just as I was prepared to die,' he said. 'Now hope is dying again. The Golden Bird will not forgive. And you must die with me, and Grue . . .'

Babka looked at the fire glowing in the iron pot, still burning brightly but never consumed.

Without its warmth they would never have survived so long.

'I cannot believe the Golden Bird has deserted us,' she replied firmly.

Chapter Thirteen

Babka and the Wolves

The blizzard raged for seven days and then died down. Their food was all eaten and Grue pined, thin and miserable. Babka ventured out of the snow shelter when the wind stopped, leading Grue, and he started to scrape away the snow with his hoofs looking for the thin wiry grass of the plain. Babka remembered the berries on the bushes and she began to search also. She found a handful still fresh and sweet under their frozen coverlet and took them to the King.

'They look like drops of blood,' he said, eating them greedily, and starting to look for more. He was still very weak in the legs, for there had been little room in the shelter for him to exercise them, and once or twice he stumbled in the snow.

'Now the blizzard is over you must take Grue, your Majesty, and ride to Bonno's cave. She will feed you and Grue until your strength returns and then you will be able to make your way to the city if the Prince has not already found you,' said Babka.

'We must all go. I cannot leave you here to starve,' replied the King.

'Grue is too weak to carry both of us. Walking would take too long. You are the King. It is best you should go,' replied Babka firmly.

But when the King mounted Grue the little pony trotted a few yards and then collapsed. There was no strength in him.

'You must go on foot, Babka. You are the strongest. You must go and bring help,' said the King.

'What will you live on while I'm gone?' asked Babka.

'Grue and I will search for berries and grass under the snow. You must take your iron pot with its fire and your feather cloak to keep you warm, otherwise you will die of cold at night. I shall gather the dead bushes to keep a fire in the shelter. And I will make you some snowshoes so that you'll be able to walk over the snow more easily.'

It seemed the only thing to do, and Babka agreed.

'But how will you find your way?' asked the King, looking out at the flat white desolation.

'By the north star,' replied Babka. 'It guided me here and it will show me the way back to Bonno's cave. By keeping it behind me I shall know if I'm going in the right direction. As soon as it appears I will set off, for the longer I wait the weaker we'll become.'

She busied herself collecting twigs and dead bushes so that the King would have a fire, while he made the snowshoes as best he could. As soon as the star appeared in the sky she set off wrapped in her feather cloak and carrying the iron pot in her hand. Her heart was heavy when she said good-bye to the King and Grue, but she appeared calm and cheerful and the King was the same. Only poor Grue drooped his head and would not be consoled. He wanted to go with her.

Babka found the snowshoes clumsy at first, but she soon found out how to walk in them and began to make good progress. By the time the star had faded she had covered several miles and could no longer see the rock. Scooping out a small shelter in a snow bank she sat down to rest. Without her feather cloak and fire she would have frozen to the ground.

When she set off again the sky had clouded and the star

kept hiding behind wisps of cloud. What would she do if the clouds thickened and she could not see the star? And after she had been walking a little while the sky grew dim and the star disappeared behind a grey wall. 'Now I'm lost,' thought Babka. 'And the King is lost. He and poor Grue will die of cold and hunger and I shall die here alone away from the forest and the birds.'

It was useless to go on walking without the star to guide her. She knew she would only walk in a circle and exhaust herself. She sat down in the snow, warming herself with the glowing brand in the iron pot, wondering what to do next.

As she sat numb with weariness and despair she heard the sound of breathing and smelt a rank animal smell. She looked up and saw a small grey wolf standing by her side, a gaunt animal with yellow fangs and a lolling tongue.

'How did you get here?' he asked, grinning hungrily.

'How did you?' asked Babka in reply.

'I live hereabouts,' answered the wolf. 'I saw what looked like a grey bird crouching in the snow and came to see what it was and found only an old woman,' he went on in a grumbling voice.

'Do you know the way to the Lake of the Wild Geese?' asked Babka eagerly.

'Yes. But I can't go there. It's the territory of my brother, White Wolf, and if he found me on his land he would kill me.'

'But you could show me the way to go?' asked Babka.

'There are no landmarks you would recognize. I'll take you as far as I can, but I expect to be paid for my trouble.'

'Paid,' faltered Babka. 'I've nothing to give you. The King will pay you handsomely if you come to the palace.'

'I think I'll eat you instead. I'm very hungry,' replied the little grey wolf, showing his teeth.

'I'm old and skinny. I shouldn't be good to eat,' said Babka quickly.

'No. You'd not be good to eat. You're nothing but a bag of old bones and a bunch of petticoats. Give me your feather cloak to make a warm nest to sleep in and I'll take you as far as I can.'

'Perhaps the sky will have cleared by then,' thought Babka hopefully, getting up.

So she made a bargain with the wolf. He was to have the cloak when they reached the border of the White Wolf's territory.

They walked on together for several miles. Babka found it difficult to keep up with the wolf's loping strides but she struggled on. She tried to make friends with her companion and once she put her hand out as if to stroke him, but he moved away quickly and snarled. At last he stopped and sniffed the air uneasily.

'My brother, White Wolf, is not far away. Give me the feather cloak and I'll be off.'

Babka gave him the cloak and he snatched it from her and was off before she could thank him. It was growing lighter now and Babka made herself a shelter of snow, crouching low over her fire to keep warm. Without her cloak she felt she would never sleep but after a while she fell into an uneasy doze, and so she spent the time until evening came.

The star was still hidden behind the clouds. Should she walk on or wait? Had she turned round when she dozed and was she facing in the right direction? Her strength was beginning to flag and she dare not waste what little remained.

Then out of the cold mist came a wolf with pricked ears and waving tail. His yellow eyes gleamed and his upper lip was drawn back showing two broken fangs. His dirty white

coat was staring and ragged. He was almost as large as Grue.

'Do you know the way to the Lake of the Wild Geese?' asked Babka, trying not to sound afraid.

'I do,' replied the White Wolf sullenly.

'Will you show me the way?'

'What will you give me?' growled the wolf.

'I've nothing to give you. But the King will pay you well.'

'The King,' snorted the wolf. 'He used to hunt me and my family. He'll give me nothing but death.'

The wolf came nearer and sniffed the iron pot where the fire burned with a bright yellow light.

'If you weren't such a bag of bones I'd eat you. But my teeth are worn out and I can't crunch bones any more. Give me the iron pot and I'll show you the way to the Lake of the Wild Geese.'

Babka looked at the iron pot and its fire and thought of the Golden Bird and how he would never forgive her if she gave away his gift. Then she thought of the King and Grue waiting in the shelter for her to bring them help.

'Take me to where I can see Bonno's cave and you shall have the pot and the fire,' she said.

'Let me carry the pot. I'll go faster with it warming my old bones,' said the wolf craftily.

'You shall have it when I see the cave,' replied Babka.

'I can take it and run away and then you'll never find the cave, but starve to death in the snow,' retorted the wolf.

'If you do the fire will go out,' replied Babka. 'It is a magic fire.'

The wolf growled uneasily. 'You must hurry. I've no time to waste,' he said, and began to run across the snow.

Babka ran after him. Now she knew the cave was not far away her courage returned, and after a few minutes, seeing he could not tire her, the White Wolf slackened his pace.

The fire in the pot fascinated him, but Babka could see he was also afraid of it, for once when she stumbled the pot swung round and the hot side burned his rump so that he leaped away in terror.

'Take hold of my tail. It will help you along,' he said.

Babka thanked him gratefully and they covered many miles in this way before dawn. The sky was clearing and on the far horizon she thought she could see the rocks around Bonno's cave looming out of the mist. She kept her eyes on them and it seemed that the shapes were moving and coming towards them.

'Can you see anything ahead, White Wolf?' she asked.

'My eyes are old and bleared. I see nothing,' replied the wolf.

The shapes grew less shadowy. Babka became certain they were moving towards them.

'Look again, White Wolf,' she said, and this time the wolf stopped, sat on his haunches and sniffed the air.

'I smell horses and dogs and men. You're leading me to my death, old woman,' he screamed. 'How can there be men and dogs and horses on the plain in winter if they are not hunting wolves?'

'They are coming to rescue the King,' replied Babka. 'I shall tell them how you've helped me. And they will give you food.'

'They won't listen to you, old woman, when they see a wolf, for it's the nature of man to hunt us. So give me my reward and I'll be off.'

He put his nose into the iron pot as if to pick it up with his teeth, and the smouldering brand suddenly burst into flame, singeing his fur. With a snarl of fright he turned and ran away, while Babka stumbled on to meet the rescue party.

Chapter Fourteen

The Rescue

The Prince and Janek in the first sleigh came galloping towards Babka, waving and shouting.

'Babka! Babka! Where is the King?' they called as they came nearer.

'Put me on the sleigh and I'll tell you as we go! If we hurry we should be in time. My footprints will guide us. You can see them winding across the snow. Drive due north. The King is sheltering under a rock many miles from here,' panted Babka, climbing into the sleigh.

The rest of the party now came up to them. There were sledges loaded with food and fuel, servants and teams of dogs and a guide who knew the plain.

With wild cries of encouragement to their teams they set off. Janek wrapped Babka in a fur robe and made her drink some cordial, for she was shivering with cold and excitement. And as they sped over the snow Babka told her story. The Prince and Janek would have asked more questions but all she could say was 'Faster! Faster!' once she had told them briefly what had happened. The air was filled with the jingling of bells, the cracking of whips and the shouts of the drivers urging on their teams. Babka rejoiced at the noise. It would carry over the great plain and the King and Grue might hear it and know that help was coming. It would give them the will to live a little longer.

The miles Babka had walked so painfully were quickly

swallowed up. It was like a dream, thought Babka, this swift smooth ride over the snow, a good dream if the King and Grue were still living at the end of it.

The rock appeared, a small dark speck at first, then becoming more distinct. Once they had seen it the efforts of the drivers were redoubled. They shouted and cracked their whips, and the teams of dogs, urged on by the rising excitement, went all out, the snow flying under their feet, the sleighs rocking from side to side as they dashed along. The Prince was the only silent one. Babka knew he was wondering if they would find the King alive, but Babka had no more fears. The Golden Bird would not fail her at this last hour.

It was the Prince who first saw the two small figures standing by the rock. It was the King with Grue supporting him, trying to wave a welcome. Before Janek could pull his team to a standstill the Prince was out of the sleigh and running towards his father.

The rest of the party began to unload the sledges. Babka went to Grue and fed him with the cake Janek had given her.

'We'll soon be back in the forest,' she whispered in his ear, and Grue whickered with joy.

While they all rested and feasted Janek told Babka the news from the palace.

'I rode away to find the Prince as soon as I knew the Queen was dead. We were riding back together when Krak gave us the message from Bonno. We organized the search party at once and set out to find you. When the people knew the King was found and alive they went mad with joy. The members of the Queen's party fled. There will be no more trouble from them.'

'The magician? The King will have no mercy on him. Yet he helped me,' said Babka anxiously.

Janek shrugged his shoulders. 'He's dead. The Queen poisoned him as she lay dying. She sent for him to drink a last cup of wine with her. He knew it was poisoned but he drank it. What does it matter? He has gone and the Prince is my master, which suits me better. Now I shall make my way in the world.'

'It's what you deserve, Janek. But for your quickness the King might now be dead,' replied Babka.

'I wanted to save you as well, Babka,' said Janek. 'And you've not done so badly. The Prince will never forget you saved the King.'

'We must thank the Golden Bird also,' replied Babka.

The King was anxious to return to the palace as quickly as possible. They journeyed in stages, stopping to camp one night by Bonno's cave and then on to Nonno's hut in the forest.

When they arrived there Babka asked the King if she might leave the party and return alone to her own little house. She felt a great longing to sit once more in the sun outside her hut making her brooms. She was weary of the long distances she had gone.

'Why do you want to leave us?' asked the King. 'I had hoped you would make your home in the palace. You shall have a respected place at court, your own apartments, a carriage, a garden of your own, anything you ask for.'

'I have everything I need in the forest,' replied Babka.

Reluctantly the King consented to let her go. But first she must share in the welcome his people were preparing.

'You must be with us on our triumphant day,' he said firmly.

'As you command, your Majesty,' returned Babka, making a deep curtsey of obedience.

The sun was shining brilliantly as the cavalcade arrived at the outskirts of the city. They were met by crowds dressed in their best clothes and shouting with joy. Children carried baskets of leaves and flower petals to strew before them. There was dancing, the wide skirts of the women whirling like gay-looking tops, the men playing their pipes and fiddles, the knots of red ribbons on their hats and shoulders fluttering like banners. Drummers in scarlet coats beat their drums. It was a wonderful occasion.

Babka was very proud to be part of it. She was happy also because the people no longer looked gaunt with famine and fear. The Prince had given orders that the palace storehouses be opened and food and seed corn given to the people, while the great herds of cattle and horses belonging to the Queen had been shared out among those who had lost their animals in the famine. Everyone was working

with renewed hope. There were some who said that the death of the Queen had removed an evil spell from the land.

Babka rode on Grue behind the King and the Prince. Grue had a red saddlecloth, bells on his shining harness and his neat little hoofs were polished until they shone. He stepped out as proudly as the King's charger and the white horse of the Prince. Babka still wore her blue skirt and flowered jacket and apron. She had refused to be dressed in silks and satins.

'Let me be as I am,' she had begged the King. Janek, however, had placed on her shoulders a fine blue cloak lined with scarlet, and this she had accepted.

As they came to the palace gates Grue suddenly tossed his head and whickered excitedly. Babka looked up and there was the Golden Bird magnificent in his crimson and gold plumage circling above them.

'All will be well now,' Babka said to herself. The King had also seen the Golden Bird and he turned and looked at her and both of them were filled with thankfulness because the Golden Bird had blessed the home-coming.

Chapter Fifteen

The Return of the Nut Maiden

The day after the return of the King, Babka was allowed to slip away quietly as the King had promised. Grue was to take her, and when Babka went to the courtyard she found Janek filling Grue's saddlebags.

'In a few days I will come and take Grue back to Nonno,' he said. 'I wish you would let me come with you today,' he added.

Babka smiled at him. 'I want to go alone. I like it best that way. But I shall always be pleased to see you, Janek,' she said.

He showed her one bag filled with oats for Grue, the other filled with sausage, cheese, butter and other provisions for herself. Babka was touched by his thoughtfulness. She had slipped a few crusts left from her breakfast into her apron pocket, knowing there would be no food in the hut.

'You could have had the bags filled with gold,' Janek said. 'Why did you refuse?'

'It will not be long before I've made some brooms to sell,' replied Babka mildly. 'What would I do with gold in the forest? It would attract robbers and other greedy people. As it is nobody will harm me for what I possess.'

Janek scratched his head. He could think of many things to buy with a bag of gold.

When Babka had left the palace well behind and was in

the forest she was surprised to find the Prince waiting for
her.

His face was very sad and she knew he was thinking of
Wanda, the nut maiden, his lost love. Babka had hoped that
now the King had returned the Prince would not resume his
wanderings looking for the nut maiden.

'One last time, Babka,' the Prince said quietly. 'Then I
will give up the search. Let me come with you through the
forest.'

They rode on in silence. Babka could think of nothing to
comfort him.

As they came nearer her little house Babka noticed small
birds beginning to gather about them, dipping and rising
and fluttering in their path. 'They are leading you home,
like the people who welcomed us yesterday,' remarked the
Prince.

Remembering how forlorn the clearing and her little
house had been when she left it to look for the Grey
Gander, Babka was prepared to find it still desolate. To her
surprise and delight the grass was fresh and green, the little
fountain playing, the vegetable patch newly dug and
weeded, while by the door was a new chopping block and
piles of logs ready to burn. Only one thing was lacking. The
little chestnut tree had disappeared.

Babka looked at the Prince but he shook his head.

'I gave no orders...' he began, and then shouted excitedly, 'Look! Someone is living in your hut. Smoke is
coming out of the chimney and the door is opening.'

The Prince dismounted quickly but Babka was already
running towards the door. A girl was standing there, with
long shining chestnut-brown hair falling in two heavy
braids over her shoulders. It was Wanda, the nut maiden.

'Babka! Babka!' she cried. 'You've come home.'

Then she saw the Prince and she cried out again, 'I knew

Babka would bring you. The long days of waiting are over!'

For a while they could do nothing but look at each other and embrace, laughing and crying with happiness. But at last they grew calmer and Wanda told her story.

When the Queen's death had released her from the spell which had made her disappear she had found herself alone outside Babka's hut, with all around her the desolation caused by the angry mob when the white cow disappeared. Going into the hut to look for Babka she found it empty and neglected, the fire out, the stools still overturned.

At first she had wandered about the forest seeking Babka, afraid to go to the village lest the people were unfriendly, until starving and exhausted she returned to the hut to die.

It was Joseph who had saved her. He had come seeking Babka to bring her food. Both he and Anna had been suffering from a fever brought on by the famine, but as soon as he was strong enough he had come to the hut, fearful of what he might find, for he had heard of the dreadful happenings on the day the Queen and her men had tried to burn Babka for a witch.

Instead of Babka he had found Wanda in the hut. He had given her food and Anna had helped her to make the hut clean and neat again. Joseph had chopped the wood and worked in the garden making everything as it had been before. He had been certain Babka would come back to them and wanted everything to be ready for her.

'Joseph knew you would come back. And he was right,' Wanda said.

As she finished speaking they heard Joseph's voice calling excitedly. He gasped when he saw Babka and the Prince.

'I came to bring you good news, Wanda, but I see you know it already,' he said, after bowing low to the Prince and kissing his hand.

The Prince embraced him warmly.

'Your Highness.... The honour is too great....' Joseph stuttered.

'You saved Wanda,' returned the Prince.

'I did it for Babka,' Joseph said. And then he hugged Babka fiercely as if he would never let her go.

'Everyone in the village is so proud of you, Babka. When we heard you were at the palace with the King and the other great ones we said: "That is our Babka! There she is riding behind the King not dressed like a grand lady but like one of us." What an honour for the village! I tell you, Babka, we talk of nothing else. Excuse me, your Highness, but my tongue runs away with me ... what with the news about Babka and the King coming home.'

'We, also, are very proud of Babka,' said the Prince.

Wanda went back with the Prince, this time to live in the palace. The King said she must learn the duties of a Queen to be ready for the time when he handed over the crown to his son. Wanda tried hard and the King helped her, for he soon came to love her dearly, while the Prince, her husband, loved her more than ever, if that were possible. They still kept the little secret house in the palace grounds and on moonlight nights she and the Prince would steal away there together and she would dance for him under the trees as she had done when she was a nut maiden.

Sometimes with Janek in attendance they would come riding to the forest to visit Babka.

And Babka? She went on making her brooms and looking after the wild birds, and wandering in the forest picking herbs to make medicines for the villagers as she had always done. Sometimes when she took a last look at the sky before going to bed she would see a great bird sail over the clearing, his plumage aglow with light as he flew serenely into the sunset. Babka would curtsey to him, and whisper her thanks for the fire that never went out, the fountain that never ceased to flow and the beautiful forest that was her home.

There are now more than 700 Puffins to choose from,
and some of them are described
on the following pages.

Hobberdy Dick

K. M. Briggs

Long ago there was plenty of secret folk life in England, particularly hobgoblins who guarded the houses and lands and watched over the families who lived in them, until their task was done and they were released.

Hobberdy Dick of Widford Manor in the Cotswolds, was a good and careful guardian but the new family who came in after the Civil War did not win his affection like the Culvers, whom he had known and liked for two hundred years. The Puritan city merchant and his spoilt wife worked their servants hard and forbade all country pleasures. There was no mumming or Maying, or Christmas dancing or Easter egg rolling now, and none of the comfortable chat and fireside games that Dick had loved in the past.

K. M. Briggs is a well-known authority on folk lore, and Hobberdy Dick is so memorable and charming a character that this book is very well worth reading, not just for its wealth of magic and historical material but for its fascinating story.

A Book of Goblins

edited by Alan Garner

'The woman stood in the middle of the floor. She was dressed in white, and had white hair. She opened her eyes with a small stick, and the upper eyelid fell back over her head like a hat.

'"I am two hundred and ninety winters," she said, "and I serve nine masters, and the house in which you stand is haunted by demons." '

This is just one of the extraordinary beings Alan Garner has gathered in this anthology. In it you will meet such oddities as Bash Tchelik, the winged Russian demon who could overcome whole armies, and Yallery Brown, the tiny, malignant old man who brought misery on the boy who helped him, and the man of snow who wed the Red Indian chief's daughter.

Alan Garner has had a lifelong interest in myths and legends, and this collection of stories reflects both the width of his reading and his own very individual taste. An excellent book for anyone else who likes to travel a little beyond reality and enjoy a few shivers and shudders.

For readers of ten and over.

Charlotte Sometimes

Penelope Farmer

Imagine going off to boarding school for the first time and waking up to find you are in the same school, but everything else in the room has changed, you are called by a new name and are in fact a different girl living in the same school forty years earlier. Not only that but you keep switching backwards and forwards, being yourself and making friends and doing lessons in today's world and waking up for no reason to different friends and lessons right in the middle of World War One.

No wonder Charlotte got tired and confused and into trouble for calling her headmistress by the wrong names and forgot to tell her other self about the girl who was supposed to be her best friend. Charlotte you see was only Charlotte Sometimes, and however interesting it was to have two selves, she preferred being herself.

For everyone over ten but girls may enjoy it most.

Bottersnikes and Gumbles

S. A. Wakefield

Deep in the Australian bush, where the Spiny Anteater and the Kookaburra live, there are some even more unusual animals – Bottersnikes and Gumbles. Bottersnikes are ugly and are probably the laziest creatures in the whole world, so they find their homes readymade in rubbish heaps among rusty old pots and pans.

Gumbles are little creatures who love to paddle in ponds (they can't actually swim) and are hopeless when they go all giggly.

When some Bottersnikes caught some nice round little Gumbles they discovered they could squeeze them to any shape they liked without hurting them, and that if they were pressed very hard they flattened out like pancakes and couldn't get back to their proper shapes without help.

'Useful,' growled the Bottersnike King. 'We can pop 'em into jam tins and squash 'em down hard so's they can't get away, and when I want some work done they'll be ready and waiting to do it.' And so began the long, comic struggle between the Gumbles and the Bottersnikes, for the Gumbles were much too clever to stay stuck in those pesky jam tins for long.

For readers of eight and over.

A Wizard of Earthsea

Ursula Le Guin

The island of Gont, a single mountain that lifts its peak a mile above the storm-racked North-east Sea, is a land famous for wizards, and not the least famous of these was a boy called Sparrowhawk who first discovered his magic power when he defended his village against an enemy horde.

Later he was taken to Roke Island, home of the famous School for Wizards, where he grew daily in knowledge and skill, till pride tempted him to try certain dangerous powers before he was equipped to deal with them, and he let loose an evil shadow-beast in his land.

Every so often a fantasy is written which stands out from the multitude in its wisdom, its originality, and its unforgettable situations: this is such a book. It won the Hornbook Prize in 1969.

For readers of eleven and over.

Fattypuffs and Thinifers

Andre Maurois

Edmund Double loved food and was plump, like his mother, while his brother Terry could hardly wait to leave the table and was consequently very thin, like his father. Nonetheless, they were all very fond of each other and the boys were amazed when, happening by chance to take a moving staircase to the Country Under the Earth, they found themselves split up and thrust headlong into the midst of the dispute between the warring nations of the Fattypuffs and the Thinifers.

The sparkle and easy humour of Andre Maurois' book is certain to fascinate children of all ages as long as Fattypuffs and Thinifers co-exist and remain mutually indispensable.

Worzel Gummidge and Saucy Nancy

Barbara Euphan Todd

'I've always had a fancy to see the sea,' remarked Worzel when he heard John and Susan were to have their holiday at the seaside instead of Scatterbrook Farm. 'Maybe Earthy and me might come along the day arter tomorrow. Oooh Aye! Seaside, that's the name o' the place, ain't it?'

But the name of the place was Seashell, which had never entertained a pair of scarecrows before, and from the goings on that followed their arrival, it would never want to again. Mrs Bloomsbury-Barton was absolutely horrified by the song Saucy Nancy, the ship's figurehead, sang in her bath, and no-one was pleased when Earthy 'tidied up' all the clothes on the beach.

The Town That Went South

Clive King

Gargoyle the rectory cat made the Discovery on his way to his night hunting grounds; where there should have been railway lines there was only cold, choppy water. Gargoyle went straight to the Vicar, who rang the church bells for everyone to gather in the square and decide what to do about The Flood.

But it wasn't a Flood. It was something even more astonishing. The town of Ramsly had come adrift from the rest of England and was floating gently across the Channel to France. By the author of *Stig of the Dump.*

For readers of eight and over.

The Minnipins

Carol Kendall

Every good Minnipin should act exactly like the others, and have the same healthy respect for the leading family, the Periods. But Muggles, she was beginning to question the smug authority of the Periods, and to sympathise more with Gummy the poet, Curley Green the painter, and Walter the Earl, the old antiquarian. So, when the eccentrics were outlawed from the village, Muggles went with them to build a new settlement high on a mountain, and for the first time in their lives they were all happy.

Then the old enemies of the Minnipin people found their way back into the Minnipin valley, but could the exiles ever make all the people in the village believe in their danger?

The Minnipins is one of those great and wise fantasies that enrich the imagination and also help us to see our own world more clearly.

The Grey Goose of Kilnevin

Patricia Lynch

In spite of the old gander's advice: *'Don't go next or nigh a fox! Don't go pokin yer gobs into holes! Keep away from dogs. Walk on the grass. Tis aisier on the feet, an', whatever Jim Daly ses, take yer time; take yer time!'*, Betsy, the little grey goose, did not get to market with the rest. She found Sheila instead, a poor, valiant little drudge for Fat Maggie. Though this is a fairy tale, with magic and all manner of queer happenings, the story rings strangely true. It is Ireland, with ballad singers at the street corners, and market days as different from anything to be seen in London, as you can well imagine.

If you have enjoyed this book and would like to know about others which we publish, why not join the Puffin Club? You will receive the club magazine, *Puffin Post*, four times a year and a smart badge and membership book. You will also be able to enter all the competitions. For details, of cost and an application form send a stamped addressed envelope to:

The Puffin Club Dept. A
Penguin Books Limited
Bath Road,
Harmondsworth
Middlesex